	DATE DUE		
MAY 2 9 1984			
SEP 24 1998	AUG 1 6 1998		
MAY 2 8 2011			
Jan 24, 2012			

Auntie Mame

a new play by

Jerome Lawrence and Robert E. Lee

based on the novel by Patrick Dennis

with a foreword by Patrick Dennis

THE VANGUARD PRESS, NEW YORK

Auntie Mame

Having had nothing to do with writing the play *Auntie Mame,* it is easy for me to be quite detached and objective about it. And I can say, right along with the critics and the thousands of people who have seen it, that it makes a wonderfully entertaining evening in the theatre.

If you are looking for a conventional little play suitable for the Freshman Frolic or the church basement—the sort of thing summarized in the catalogues of dramatic publishers as "Comedy; one interior; modern dress; three acts; four men; five women"—keep right on looking because *Auntie Mame* isn't it.

Like Mame herself, *Auntie Mame* is in no way conventional as a play. Nor could it be, because my novel, *Auntie Mame,* from which the play is derived, isn't even a novel, really. It is, instead, a couple of dozen episodes that take place in a couple of dozen localities over a couple of dozen years. I can't quite label it myself, but the matchless Rosalind Russell, who originated the role of Mame, who *is* Mame, calls this offering "a revue without music," and her definition is better than any I can supply. Both novel and play are freaks, then—but such *popular* freaks that their lavish eccentricities cannot be entirely despised.

Not every episode in my book is in the play. To get them all in—not that every one is worth dramatizing—would require passing out box luncheons, blankets, and tooth brushes to a rough-and-ready audience of slavish theatregoers weaned on Eugene O'Neill and the Ring Series. But an astonishing number of the episodes in the book *are* in the play; enough so that the casual reader is convinced that every word of the novel has been translated to the stage. If that isn't catching the "spirit" of a book, I don't know what is.

And Jerome Lawrence and Robert E. Lee have gone yet a step further in their dramatization, for they have caught —far better than I—the moments of heartbreak that are also in *Auntie Mame* and placed them on the stage so deftly that, between the guffaws and giggles, snickers and snorts, there are audible sobs and visible tears at each and every performance. That is what I meant to do in the novel and, I am afraid, failed. To me, comedy is measured not only by its laughs, but by its tears. With every pratfall the heart should also ache. In this play it does, and I still cry just as hard when I drop into the Broadhurst Theatre now as I did on the night the play was out in Wilmington. Two handkerchiefs are par for the course.

But enough of the clown longing to play Hamlet. To quote from *Hamlet* itself, "The play's the thing something, something, something the king." And here it is, a warm, rich, sprawling, unorthodox comedy that I am proud and happy to have inspired.

PATRICK DENNIS

All the sick-rooms in America—and a large proportion of the well-rooms—are strewn with copies of Patrick Dennis' remarkable novel *Auntie Mame*. It is not easy to pin-point the lady's hypnotic fascination, but there is a fiercely familiar quality about her. Something of her determination to do, be, and see everything in human experience burbles in everyone's blood stream.

Perhaps Mame is a symbol of this century. Since the time Mr. Coolidge started getting his shirts laundered on Pennsylvania Avenue, anyone truly perceptive could absorb more interesting stimuli in an hour than a Victorian aunt might encounter in a month of bank holidays. From all the recent miracles of communication and mobility, a new kind of human being has emerged: the *multi-person*. And because Mame is the multi-person personified, we could no more squeeze her into a single set than a single snapshot could portray the limitless panorama of her life and adventures. In his novel, Patrick Dennis barely nodded in the direction of the Aristotelian unities. We determined to toss Mr. Aristotle's pronunciamentos squarely in the ash can. We deliberately set out to design an entertainment that had the scope and ubiquity to match Mame's multi-personality.

Dramatizing *Auntie Mame* was an interesting challenge, because everybody agreed on one thing: it was impossible. Of course it is, in terms of conventional theatre. But we are very lucky: we have unconventional audiences. And, we hope, unconventional readers.

Every work for the theatre requires producers with taste,

a director with resourcefulness and insight, a designer with playwright's blood, and a player who knows that it requires an equal portion of hard work and ham to create that luminescence Noel Coward calls "star quality." *Auntie Mame* has had all these in Fryer and Carr, Morton Da-Costa, Oliver Smith, and the unforgettable Rosalind Russell.

JEROME LAWRENCE

ROBERT E. LEE

AUNTIE MAME was presented by Robert Fryer and Lawrence Carr at the Broadhurst Theatre, New York City, October 31, 1956, with the following cast: (in order of appearance)

NORAH MULDOON, Beulah Garrick

PATRICK DENNIS, *age 10,* Jan Handzlik

ITO, Yuki Shimoda

RAYMOND, Cris Alexander

VERA CHARLES, Polly Rowles

RALPH DEVINE, Grant Sullivan

BISHOP ELEFTHAROSEES, William Martel

M. LINDSAY WOOLSEY, John O'Hare

AUNTIE MAME, Rosalind Russell *

MR. WALDO, *a paperhanger,* Geoffrey Bryant

MR. BABCOCK, Robert Allen

AL LINDEN, *the stage manager,* Wally Mohr

ASSISTANT STAGE MANAGER, Duane Camp

A THEATRE MANAGER, William Martel

A MAID, Kip McCardle

A BUTLER, Paul Lilly

A LEADING MAN, James Field

LORD DUDLEY, Walter Reimer

A CUSTOMER, Kip McCardle

A CUSTOMER'S SON, Barry Towsen

MR. LOOMIS, *a floor-walker,* Cris Alexander

BEAUREGARD JACKSON PICKETT BURNSIDE, Robert Smith

COUSIN JEFF, William Martel

COUSIN FAN, Nan McFarland

* Beginning January 20, 1958: Miss Greer Garson

COUSIN MOULTRIE, Frank Roberts
SALLY CATO MACDOUGAL, Marian Winters
EMORY MACDOUGAL, Barry Blake
MOTHER BURNSIDE, Ethel Cody
FRED, *a groom,* Paul Lilly
SAM, *another groom,* James Field
A HUNTSMAN, Cris Alexander
DR. SHURR, *a vet,* Geoffrey Bryant
PATRICK DENNIS, *a young man,* Robert Higgins
AGNES GOOCH, Peggy Cass
BRIAN O'BANNION, James Monks
GLORIA UPSON, Joyce Lear
DORIS UPSON, Dorothy Blackburn
CLAUDE UPSON, Walter Klavun
PEGEEN RYAN, Patricia Jenkins
MICHAEL DENNIS, Jan Handzlik

and a great many friends of AUNTIE MAME.

Entire production directed by Morton DaCosta
Production designed by Oliver Smith
Lighting by Peggy Clark
Costumes by Noel Taylor
Mame's costumes designed by Travis Banton
Production stage manager: Robert Linden

The action of the play takes place in AUNTIE MAME'S
Beekman Place apartment and various
other locales in which she becomes involved in a period
of years from 1928 to 1946.

Act One

*A projection appears on the scrim. It is a blowup of
a legal document which moves like a TV crawl as the
audience reads it:*

"LAST WILL AND TESTAMENT

I, Edwin Dennis, being of sound mind
and body, do hereby bequeath to my
only son, Patrick, all my worldly posses-
sions. In the event of my demise, I direct
our faithful servant, Norah Muldoon, to
deliver Patrick to my sister and next of
kin, Mame Dennis, at 3 Beekman Place,
New York City. The expenses of his up-
bringing shall be supervised by the
Knickerbocker Bank as trustee, with the
full power to keep that crazy sister of
mine from doing anything too damned
eccentric."

Behind this rolling document, the music begins to sound a trifle fey and Disneyesque.

> "Since I keep myself in splendid physical condition through daily workouts at the Chicago Athletic Club, I am confident that these provisions will not go into force or effect for many years. I hereby affix my hand this fourteenth day of October, in the year 1928.
>
> Signed:
>
> EDWIN DENNIS"

There is a startled, eyebrow-lifting figure in the music, and the will slides out of sight, to be followed by a newspaper clipping which reads:

> "CHICAGO TRIBUNE—October 15, 1928
>
> BUSINESSMAN DROPS DEAD
> IN STEAM ROOM OF
> CHICAGO ATHLETIC CLUB"

We bleed through the scrim; silhouetted in the foyer of the Beekman Place apartment are the stiff and uncomfortable figures of NORAH MULDOON *and* PATRICK, *aged ten.*

NORAH *tentatively presses the doorbell. From the interior of the apartment we hear laughter and the muffled gaiety of a fairly well-oiled party. The foyer is decorated in the gaudy Chinoiserie of the late Twenties.*

NORAH (*looking around uncomfortably*): It's like the ladies' rest room in the Oriental The-ay-ter.

YOUNG PAT (*clutching on to* NORAH's *hand in terror*): You're not scared, are you, Norah?

NORAH: Of course not, and don't you be, Patrick. Norah's here to look after you. (*She refers to a slip of paper in her trembling hand.*) Number three, Beekman Place. This is where the lawyer told us to come. We're only doing what he told us. Of course we're not scared, child.

(*They are drinking in the strangeness of their sur-
roundings and do not notice the door as it opens.* ITO,
a diminutive Japanese houseman, pads out unheard.)

ITO: You want?

(NORAH *jumps.* PATRICK *grasps* NORAH'S *hand more
tightly.*)

NORAH: Glory be to God! I'm Miss . . . that is, I'm Norah
Muldoon. And I've been sent by this boy's father—
God rest his soul—to bring young Patrick here to live
with his aunt, Miss . . . (*She glances again at the slip
of paper.*) a Miss Mame Dennis, her name is.

(ITO *studies* NORAH, *then young* PATRICK—*still cling-
ing to* NORAH.)

ITO (*with sudden resolve*): Must be mistake. No want little
boy today.

(ITO *starts to slam the door, but* NORAH *puts her foot
in it.*)

NORAH: But I sent the wire from Chicago myself, saying
we'd arrive at six o'clock today.

ITO: Not important. Boy here, house here, Madam here.
You come in. You wait. I fetch. (*Turns.*) Madam having affair now.

(ITO *starts to usher them into the noisy interior of the
apartment.* PATRICK *looks warily at* NORAH.)

YOUNG PAT: Norah, do you think we ought to?

NORAH: We've got no choice, Paddy. We've got no place
to go.

YOUNG PAT *and* NORAH *go through the door, and the wall of the foyer breaks away, revealing a cross section of Mame's Beekman Place apartment. A dozen or more people are milling about at the inebriated apex of a cocktail party. There is apparently a dining room off right and a bar off left. The guests are continuously crossing back and forth between the hors d'oeuvres and the wet stuff.*

Upstage center is a curved staircase that ascends to a bedroom area left.

NORAH *and* YOUNG PAT *look about them, baffled by the milling confusion.*

GIRL: Oh, Alex, you're simply *murdering* me!

(The apartment is homey as a Shinto shrine—low tables, low sofas, and high guests.

Among the guests are a man who looks very much like Alexander Woollcott; a man who looks very much like Robert Benchley; RALPH DEVINE, *a muscular educator; a be-sandaled mystic who could be Raymond Duncan; an orthodox Lithuanian bishop;* M. LINDSAY WOOLSEY; *and other typical cocktail-party habitués of the late Twenties.*

VERA CHARLES, a famous British actress from Pittsburgh, is holding forth in the center of the room.

ITO motions NORAH and PAT to a bench, where they sit uncomfortably.

There is a cheery panel behind them, depicting a Japanese nobleman disemboweling himself with a samurai sword.

ITO scurries out of sight, in search of AUNTIE MAME.)

VERA: Mame's been trying to lure me into the daylight for months!—Birds and the trees and all of that horrible nature business that I can't stand till five o'clock in the afternoon.

NORAH: Motheragod, the halls of hell!

RALPH DEVINE: Go on, Vera, go on.

VERA: Well, darling, I couldn't tell you why I ever let Mame persuade me, but Isadora Duncan had persuaded Mame that a fling into modern dance would tone her up. And you'll never believe—

RADCLIFFE (*a He-type She, entering*): Well, God knows if they want Maude killed professionally, they've sent the poor slob to the right place.

VERA: Radcliffe!

NORAH: White Slavers!

RADCLIFFE: I told her from the start—

VERA: Really, Radcliffe!

RADCLIFFE: Sorry, darling. Didn't realize you were still on.

VERA: Anyway, there we were, barefooted in our camisoles on Isadora's lawn—squatting and unsquatting. Raymond, darling, you really should speak to Isadora. Of course, *I* managed beautifully—I was grace personified—but it damned near killed Mame.

RAYMOND: Isadora's whole theory of modern dance is based on challenging the pelvis.

VERA: Mame was challenged all right. She had to go to Swami Paramanda for a month to push her pelvis back where it was. (*Lowering her voice.*) Don't, for heaven's sake, mention to Mame that I mentioned this. You know, I adore her, but in a camisole—well!!!

(MAME *enters, down the stairs.*)

AUNTIE MAME: I'll get the maid started, Ito. Ring up Bonelli and tell him to get out here with some more gin. (AUNTIE MAME's *hair is bobbed very short with straight bangs above her slanting brows; a long robe of embroidered golden silk floats out behind her. She wears tiny gold slippers twinkling with jewels, and jade and ivory bracelets clatter on her arms. Her long fingernails are lacquered a delicate green. An almost endless bamboo cigarette holder hangs languidly from her bright red mouth. She crosses to* NORAH *and looks at her with an expression of bemused surprise.*) Oh, dear, the Employment Bureau didn't tell me you were bringing a child with you. Well, no matter. He looks like a nice little boy. And if he misbehaves, we can always toss him into the river. (*All laugh, except* NORAH *and* YOUNG PAT.) I guess you know what's expected of you—just a little light slavery around the place.

NORAH: I'm prepared to *buy* my way out. I'll give you my life savings if you'll let this child and me escape from this nest of thieves and slayers!

(AUNTIE MAME *reacts with sad incredulity, then plucks at the sleeve of a distinguished man wearing a goatee.*)

AUNTIE MAME: Dr. Fuchtwanger—just in time. You'd better get this woman on your couch in a hurry.

NORAH: I'm not that kind of a woman, Mum. All I'm looking for is a Miss Mame Dennis who's supposed to live at Number three, Beekman Place.

AUNTIE MAME (*calling*): Ito, oh, Ito!

(ITO *comes on.*)

Ito, where have you been? Show this woman the kitchen and get her started on the glasses.

ITO: Oh, Missy Dennis, this not dishwashing lady.

AUNTIE MAME: Oh, I'm so sorry. (*Shrugs.*) Then I must have invited you. What would you like to drink?

NORAH: Did you not get my telegram? I'm Norah Muldoon.

AUNTIE MAME (*gasps*): No! That's not possible. The wire said December first. That's tomorrow. This is November thirty-first.

NORAH (*balefully*): No, Mum. 'Tis the first, God curse the evil day.

AUNTIE MAME: That's ridiculous. Everyone knows "Thirty days hath September, April, June and Nov—" Oh, God! (*Dramatically she enfolds* YOUNG PAT *in her arms.*) But darling! *I'm* your Auntie *Mame!* (*Baffled,* YOUNG PAT *submits to* AUNTIE MAME'S *effusive embrace. She turns toward her guests, lifting her voice.*) Quiet, quiet, everybody. I have an important announcement to make. This is *my little boy.* (*There are reactions of surprise, pleasure, and a few raised eyebrows.*) Oh, he's not really *my* little boy. He's my brother's son. From Chicago. (*She sniffs.*) My poor late brother. (NORAH *crosses herself. There are some sympathetic clucks and one hiccup.*) This little tyke. In all the whole wide world, I'm his only living relative. And he's my only living relative. (*She stoops down and embraces him again.*) That's all we have, just each other, my little love. (*There are a few moist eyes at this touching scene. Then* MAME *looks at* YOUNG PAT *quizzically.*) What's your—(*Recovers.*) What am I going to call you, dear?

YOUNG PAT: Pat. Patrick Dennis.

AUNTIE MAME: I know the Dennis part, darling, and from now on you must call me "Auntie Mame." Now, how would you like a mart—? Is it your bedtime? Heavens, it can't be. Do you want the . . . ah, powder room, darling? Or food? Food, that's it! You must be famished. You run right along in there and help yourself to the caviar—(PAT *starts toward the inside room right. She calls after him.*) After that you can go up and read a book or something.

RALPH DEVINE (*approaching* MAME): Oh, Mame! You're not going to let that child *read?* Taste life second-hand!

AUNTIE MAME: Ralph, do you think you could work little Patrick into one of your advanced study groups?

RALPH DEVINE: Yes, I think there just might be an opening.

(PAT *returns, munching a deviled egg.*)

AUNTIE MAME (*to* YOUNG PAT): Where've you been going to school, dear?

YOUNG PAT: Chicago Boys' Latin.

RALPH DEVINE (*with a hollow laugh*): Uh-huh. Where they build a wall of dull encyclopedias around the id!

YOUNG PAT: The id?

RALPH DEVINE: See? Doesn't even know a simple two-letter world. That's John Dewey for you.

AUNTIE MAME (*explaining to* YOUNG PAT): Shake hands with Mr. Devine, Patrick. He runs a school down in the Village where they do all sorts of advanced things. Perhaps we'll enroll you there.

YOUNG PAT (*eagerly, shaking hands with* RALPH): Is it a military school? Do they wear uniforms?

(RALPH DEVINE *looks appalled.*)

RALPH DEVINE: In my school, young man, we don't wear *any*thing.

AUNTIE MAME: It's heaven! (NORAH *is shocked, but* ITO *tugs her out of the room, up the stairs. The party begins to bubble again.* MAME *draws* YOUNG PAT *aside.*) Now, these are a lot of your Auntie Mame's *closest* friends;

I don't know all their names, but you can just circu-
late and you'll hear the most fascinating conversation.
Oh, I'm sorry you missed the cast of the *Blackbirds,*
but they had to leave early.

YOUNG PAT: Who's he? (*He indicates the bearded patri-
arch, in mitered cap and jeweled robes, impassively
eating stuffed celery.*)

AUNTIE MAME: That's a Lithuanian bishop. Doesn't speak
a word of English. Stimulating man. (*They come into
the circle where* VERA CHARLES *is holding forth.*) Vera?
Vera, this is my little boy. Patrick! I want you to meet
a star. One of the great ladies of the theater, and your
Auntie Mame's dearest friend, Vera Charles.

YOUNG PAT: Hello.

VERA: How do you do.

AUNTIE MAME: She just *loves* little boys.

VERA (*distastefully*): Yes.

(ITO *helps the* BISHOP *into his cape.* AUNTIE MAME
moves toward him.)

AUNTIE MAME: Oh, Bishop, do you have to run? I'm so
sorry. We certainly enjoyed your conversation. Too
bad nobody else here spoke Lithuanian. (*The* BISHOP
exits, and MAME *turns, bubbling, to* RAYMOND.) Such
a darling—and so worldly for a man of God. (*She
crosses back to* YOUNG PATRICK, *who has been listening
to* VERA. AUNTIE MAME *takes his hand and draws the
boy away.*) Isn't she scintillating, darling? Now I want
you to meet—

YOUNG PAT: Auntie Mame, what's "nymphomania?"

AUNTIE MAME: It's very simple. Nymphomania is . . . (*She goes to a table, takes out pad and pencil.*) I'll tell you what we're going to do. Every time you hear a word you don't understand, just take this pad and pencil and write it down. Later on Auntie Mame will explain it to you. (YOUNG PAT *moves to take down words.*) Oh, the adventure of molding a new little life.

RAYMOND: Good-by, Mame, I've got to fly.

AUNTIE MAME: Good-by, Raymond, darling. I'll see you on Tuesday. Don't catch cold. (RAYMOND *exits. She notices* YOUNG PAT *writing.*) Are you enjoying yourself, dear?

YOUNG PAT: I guess so.

AUNTIE MAME: I imagine it's a little confusing—after Chicago and everything.

YOUNG PAT: I guess so, ma'am.

AUNTIE MAME: Uh-uh.

YOUNG PAT: I mean Auntie Mame.

AUNTIE MAME (*turning to* RALPH): Oh, dear, this is tougher than talking with the Lithuanian bishop.

(RALPH DEVINE *looks analytically at* YOUNG PAT.)

RALPH DEVINE: You know why. The poor little fella's a mass of inhibitions. Send him to me. Won't be a repression left after the first semester.

AUNTIE MAME: Consider him enrolled.

RALPH DEVINE: Good. Give his libido a good shaking up, that's what we'll do. Incidentally, Mame, how's *your* libido these days?

AUNTIE MAME: Stirred, but not shaken.

RALPH DEVINE: Who's the lucky man?—still Lindsay Woolsey?

AUNTIE MAME (*airily*): Among others.

RALPH DEVINE: Well, I wouldn't mind being one of the others that he's among.

AUNTIE MAME: You're a naughty boy, Ralph, but you have lovely muscles.

RALPH DEVINE: Well, I don't mean to drink and dash— but I don't want to be late for my rubdown.

(RALPH DEVINE *departs athletically.* VERA *is carried across in a prone position, with* ITO *at one end and* LINDSAY *supporting the great actress's feet.* VERA *is out stone-cold.*)

ITO: Guest room again, Missy?

AUNTIE MAME: No . . . no, the coats are in there. Dump her in my room. And, Ito, get that God-awful dress off her.

ITO (*grinning*): Me tuck her in.

(*He giggles as they carry her up the stairs.* AUNTIE MAME *glances at her watch.*)

AUNTIE MAME: Well, she toppled ten minutes early today. Unless there's too much juniper in the gin.

(*The* BENCHLEY *character starts out.*)

ROBERT: That's my cue, Mame. As Vera goes, so goes the party!

AUNTIE MAME: Good-by, Robert dear. I know you have a review to do tonight. Don't work too hard. (*To an-*

other guest who is departing.) Good-by, Frank. See you Tuesday at the Algonquin.

(*They go out.*)

YOUNG PAT: Is the English lady dead, Auntie Mame?

AUNTIE MAME: She's not English, darling. She's from Pittsburgh.

YOUNG PAT: She *sounded* English.

AUNTIE MAME: When you're from Pittsburgh, you've got to do something. Now, read me the words you didn't understand.

YOUNG PAT (*clearing his throat, reads with difficulty*): Free love. Stinko. Hotsy-Totsy Club. Bathtub gin. Karl Marx. (*He looks up innocently.*) Is he one of the Marx Brothers?

AUNTIE MAME: No, dear.

YOUNG PAT (*resuming*): Narciss-iss-istic. Lys-iss-istrata. Lesbian. Son-of-a—

(*Deftly* MAME *rips the page from the pad.*)

AUNTIE MAME: My, my, what an eager little mind. (*She crumbles the paper.*) You won't need some of these words for *months* and months.

(LINDSAY WOOLSEY *comes down the stairs.*)

LINDSAY: Well, I suppose the new arrival means you can't have dinner with me tonight.

AUNTIE MAME: You're so understanding, Lindsay.

LINDSAY: Displaced by the younger generation!

AUNTIE MAME: Not at all. Not at all.

LINDSAY: I suppose this means I'll be seeing you even less.

AUNTIE MAME: *More,* Lindsay, more. We'll be taking the little lad to the zoo and the aquarium—and we'll be dropping in your office and you can show him how you publish books. We'll be together almost constantly—the three of us.

LINDSAY: Yeah. That's exactly what I had in mind. (LINDSAY *exits.*)

(*The party is thinning out now. Between leave-takings,* AUNTIE MAME *tries to make her new little visitor seem at home.*)

AUNTIE MAME: Well now, there's so much we have to discover about each other. I never had a live little boy around the place before. I did mean to have your bedroom all fixed up for you. A friend of mine is coming in to re-do the sculpture room into a nursery . . . well, it's not really a sculpture room, darling, but a sculptor-friend of mine stayed in it for about six months. Such talented fingers, but what he did to my bust—uh—that's the head, you know. Anyway, he's going to re-do the room for you with bunnies all over everything.

(*A* MAN *approaches* AUNTIE MAME. *He is supporting a woman who is completely stoned.*)

MAN: 'Night, Mame. Thanks. (*He extends his hand.*)

AUNTIE MAME: Good night, Charles. (*The girl begins to topple over.*) Watch it, Edna.

MAN (*as he staggers out with his companion*): We're already late for Clifton's party. (*They go.*)

AUNTIE MAME (*calling after them*): Give Clifton my love.

Tell him I'm sorry to miss it, but to ring me up next week some time. (*To* YOUNG PAT, *leading him to the sofa.*) Now, let's sit down for one minute and really get to know each other. What did you think of the conversation at the party?

YOUNG PAT: Some of it was a little over my head.

AUNTIE MAME: Good heavens, child, didn't your father ever talk to you?

YOUNG PAT: Hardly ever. I only saw him at breakfast-time.

AUNTIE MAME: Well, what did he say then?

YOUNG PAT: He usually said, "Pipe down, kid, the old man's hung."

AUNTIE MAME: Amen. (*Turning to* YOUNG PAT.) What did you do in Chicago for *fun?*

YOUNG PAT: Well, Norah took me to the movies every Saturday afternoon. And I played parchesi with the doorman once in a while—until he got fired.

AUNTIE MAME: Oh, dear. Didn't they ever do anything cultural for you in Chicago? (*Waving it away.*) Never mind. (*She pats his cheek.*) Ahhh, your Auntie Mame is going to open doors for you, Patrick—doors you never even dreamed existed! What times we're going to have! (*She rises and crosses to a table up center, snapping off the overhead light.*) Now, what on earth did I do with that will? (*Searching through a random stack of papers in the drawer.*) It's here someplace. (*Reading from a blue-backed document.*) Five pounds Beluga caviar, get hair done—(*She turns it over.*) Oh, yes, this *is* it. (AUNTIE MAME *returns to sit beside* YOUNG PAT *on the bench and leafs through the legal document*.) Your father says you're to be reared as a Protestant. Well, I've no objection to that. (*She gazes off at the ceiling, drawing on her cigarette*.) Though it would be a shame to deprive you of the exquisite mysteries of the Eastern religions. (*She turns to him*.) Where did you go to church, darling?

YOUNG PAT: The Fourth Presbyterian.

AUNTIE MAME: You mean to say there are *four* Presbyterian churches in a place like Chicago? Well, no matter. I guess we can scrounge around and find some sort of Presbyterian church in the neighborhood. (*She continues to flip through the document*.) Now there's a lot of folderol about the Knickerbocker Bank and some Mr. Babcock who's been appointed your trustee. (*She slaps the will down on her lap, annoyed*.) Well, I see what that means. *I* have the responsibility, and your trustee has the authority.

YOUNG PAT: I saw a movie once about a trustee.

AUNTIE MAME: Oh?

YOUNG PAT: There was a big prison break, and the trustee saved the warden's daughter.

AUNTIE MAME: This isn't the kind of a trustee that lives in a prison, dear. As a rule. (*She mouths the name distastefully*.) Mr. Babcock. (*Her nostrils dilate slightly*.) We'll tackle him in our own good time. (*Tosses the will on the floor*.) Now, tell me, Patrick. Is your Auntie Mame anything like you expected?

YOUNG PAT: No, ma'am. The only picture I ever saw of you was with a shawl and a rose between your teeth. Like a Spanish lady. It's in my suitcase that's coming.

(AUNTIE MAME *smiles reminiscently; then seriously.*)

AUNTIE MAME: But didn't your father ever *say* anything— *tell* you anything—about me, before he died?

YOUNG PAT: Yes, ma'am.

AUNTIE MAME: Well, what was it? (YOUNG PAT *gulps.*) Come now, my little love. You must always be perfectly frank with your Auntie Mame.

YOUNG PAT (*takes a deep breath, and blurts it out*): Well, my father said since you're my only living relative, beggars can't be choosers. But to be left in your hands was a fate he wouldn't wish on a *dog!*

AUNTIE MAME (*evenly*): That bastard. (*Dutifully,* YOUNG PAT *reaches for the pad of foolscap and starts to write down the strange word. She glances at the boy and speaks sweetly.*) That word, dear, was "bastard." (*She takes the pad and pencil from* YOUNG PAT, *and prints in virulent block letters.*) B-A-S-T-A-R-D—(*Magnificently she hands him the pad.*) And it means *your late father!*

(*Quickly the lights fade.*)

The foyer of AUNTIE MAME'S *apartment, two weeks later.*

A PAPERHANGER *atop a ladder is putting some finishing touches on the wild, neo-Cubist wallpaper that he has just hung. He comes down the ladder, looking at his handiwork suspiciously.* NORAH *comes on and makes a little gasp at the sight of the bizarre walls.*

NORAH: What is it?

PAPERHANGER: It's wallpaper. But don't look at me. I didn't pick it out, I only pasted it on. Why, is it upside down?

NORAH: No more than everything else around here, I guess. You haven't seen the boy, have you?

PAPERHANGER: Saw a kid go out 'bout a hour ago.

NORAH: Sendin' him all over the city alone. "He's got to discover New York for himself," says she. "You can't go with him, Norah. We want him to turn out to be independent, don't we?" Independent! He'll turn out to be dead under some truck.

PAPERHANGER: I've got an order here to re-do a couple of bedrooms. Can I get in?

NORAH (*sarcastically*): At two o'clock! Why, you'll be lucky to get in by five. She's still sleepin'.

PAPERHANGER: Well, I'll get started in the other bedroom then.

NORAH: Oh, you can't go in there, either!

PAPERHANGER: Why not? She ain't sleeping in two bedrooms, is she?

NORAH: Oh, no. It's the first lady of the American the-ay-ter out cold in the guest room.

PAPERHANGER: Again! What's she do, live here?

NORAH: Miss Charles don't live here. She drinks here and and she does her passin' out here. It's a wonder to me their blood hasn't turned to vinegar. Two weeks I've been here and they've had thirteen cocktail parties.

PAPERHANGER: Only thirteen in two weeks!

NORAH: They had to call one off. The bootlegger couldn't come that day. (YOUNG PAT *dashes in, carrying a model airplane.*) Thank God you're safe.

YOUNG PAT (*running off*): Where's Auntie Mame? I've got to show her something.

NORAH (*calling off*): Your Auntie Mame's still asleep.

PAPERHANGER (*unrolling an outrageously garish length of wallpaper—the motif of a bloodshot eye*): This'll wake her up.

(*The lights fade.*)

The lights come up—faintly—on AUNTIE MAME'S *plush bedroom. She is reclining on a huge bed, with a sleeping mask over her eyes.*

YOUNG PAT *bursts in the door.*

YOUNG PAT (*excitedly*): Auntie Mame! Auntie Mame! (AUNTIE MAME *is shocked into jangling wakefulness. She sits upright in bed and clutches the mask from her face.*)

AUNTIE MAME (*confused*): What is it? What happened?

YOUNG PAT: I've got something to show you. (*He opens the Venetian blinds and a shaft of bright afternoon sunlight hits* AUNTIE MAME *squarely in the face. She reels back against the pillow.*) Look! (YOUNG PAT *spins the airplane.* AUNTIE MAME *watches it with fascinated horror.*)

AUNTIE MAME: My God! *Bats!*

YOUNG PAT (*as the airplane circles in descending spirals*): It's an actual model of the *Spirit of St. Louis.* (AUNTIE

MAME *recoils from the model airplane, as it crashes into her lap.* YOUNG PAT *rushes to recover it and to explain its mechanism to* AUNTIE MAME.) See? It's got a rubber-band motor, and I whittled the body out of balsa wood, and—

(AUNTIE MAME *gestures him away, closing her eyes and holding her aching head.*)

AUNTIE MAME: Please, darling—your Auntie Mame's hung.

(YOUNG PAT *is deeply hurt by this. It's Chicago all over again. Quietly he takes the airplane and backs out of the room.*)

YOUNG PAT (*softly*): Oh, sure, Auntie Mame.

(AUNTIE MAME *is left alone with her hangover. She sits for a moment with her hands shielding her eyes from the sunlight. Gradually she realizes what she has done. Peeking through her fingers, she braves the sunlight and calls to the boy who has left her.*)

AUNTIE MAME: Patrick. Patrick—come back. (YOUNG PAT *reappears in the doorway, uncertainly.*) You know, I really am interested in all your projects. But you've got to admit, it's a bit surprising for Auntie Mame to find Mr. Lindbergh in her bedroom before breakfast. (*She squints at the light.*) Child, how can you *see* with all that light? (*Obligingly* YOUNG PAT *crosses to the window and partially closes the Venetian blinds.*) That's better. Now be a perfect angel and ask Ito to bring me a very light breakfast: black coffee and a sidecar. And you might ask him to fix something for your Aunt Vera; I think I hear her coming to in the guest room. (YOUNG PAT *starts out obediently.*) First —come and give your Auntie Mame a good-morning kiss. But gently, dear. (YOUNG PAT *approaches timidly and kisses her.*) That was lovely, darling. You'll make some lucky woman very happy someday. (*Gingerly,* AUNTIE MAME *takes the airplane model from the boy's hand and winds the propeller tentatively*.) You know, I really am fascinated by aviation. I never knew before they did it all with rubber bands. (*As she hands the airplane back to Patrick, the propeller blows in her face insolently. The telephone rings suddenly. This affects* AUNTIE MAME *like a dentist's drill at the nape of her neck.* YOUNG PAT *picks it up.*)

YOUNG PAT (*into the phone*): Hello? Miss Dennis—yes, she's here. Who's calling, please? (*Pause.*) Hold the wire. (*To* AUNTIE MAME, *covering the mouthpiece.*) It's Mr. Babcock, from the Knickerbocker Bank.

AUNTIE MAME: Oh, my God, I've been dodging him for days. (*She hesitates, then takes the phone reluctantly. Turning on the charm.*) Oh, hello, Mr. Babcock! How nice to hear your voice at long last. (YOUNG PAT *is attentive, knowing that he is at issue here.*) I, too, am looking forward with anticipation to meeting *you.* (*She listens.*) Oh, the little lad is fine. Just fine. And he, too, can't *wait* to meet you. (YOUNG PAT *shrugs indifferently.* AUNTIE MAME *covers the mouthpiece and speaks hoarsely to* PAT.) Hurry my tray, dear. Auntie needs fuel. (YOUNG PAT *exits.* AUNTIE MAME *turns back to the phone.*) Please *do* stop by, Mr. Babcock—*any* time. (*She goes pale.*) In how many minutes? (*Flustered.*) Yes, Fifty-seventh Street is right in my, uh, "neck of the woods." "Spitting distance." How vivid. (*Pause.*) Come right along. Then you can join me for breakfa—*tea!* (*Nodding.*) Number three, Beekman Place. Right away. (*She puts down the phone. She lets out a plaintive yell.*) Vera! VERA! Get in here!

(*The door to the adjoining bedroom is opened fumblingly, and* VERA *staggers into the room.* VERA'S *evening gown looks as if it had been slept in, which it has. She still wears a totally discouraged orchid. She has one shoe on, and her hair and make-up are a mess.*)

VERA (*wobbly and incoherent*): Did you call me, darling?

AUNTIE MAME: I'm about to be attacked by the Knickerbocker Bank.

VERA: That's lovely. Why in hell did that Japanese sandman let me sleep in my best Lanvin?

AUNTIE MAME: He tried to get it off you, but you bit him. Patrick's trustee is on his way over here.

VERA: It's ruined. Absolutely ruined.

AUNTIE MAME: Some hideous creature who's coming here to thwart all the plans I've made for the boy's cultural enlargement!

VERA (*incredulously*): He's coming here—in the middle of the night? (VERA *blinks at the partially opened blinds.*) My God, that moon's bright.

AUNTIE MAME: Oh, don't be silly, Vera. Don't you realize

—some horrible man is descending like a vulture to rob me of my child?

VERA: Mame, you're being *utterly* hysterical.

AUNTIE MAME: I've got to make the right impression. You have no idea how conservative the Knickerbocker Bank is; it's so conservative they don't pay any interest at *all*.

(VERA *slaps herself in the face to waken herself as* MAME *struggles into her negligée and slippers.*)

VERA: All right. Let's get organized. What time is it? What *day* is it? (VERA *picks up a bedside clock and looks at it in horror.*) Blessed mother of Maude Adams, I was due at the Theatre Guild an hour ago.

AUNTIE MAME: You can't desert me in my predicament, Vera. Look at my face. What on earth am I going to wear? (AUNTIE MAME *starts hauling clothes out of a closet frantically and dumping them on the bed.*

VERA, *paying no attention to* MAME, *looks at herself in a hand mirror and is shocked at what she sees.*)

VERA: How am I going to face the Theatre Guild? The way I look I couldn't even understudy a witch in *Macbeth*.

AUNTIE MAME: That's just like you, Vera! Here my life is about to be blown to bits, and all you can think of is your career! (MAME *pulls out one very flashy dress, beads and spangles, and holds it up in front of herself appraisingly.*) Will this make me look like a Scarsdale matron?

(VERA *cranes forward, squinting—her eyes only a few inches from the glittering fabric.*)

VERA: Have you ever *been* to Scarsdale?

(YOUNG PAT *enters with a small breakfast tray on which there are a cup of coffee and a sidecar.*)

YOUNG PAT: Good afternoon, Auntie Vera.

VERA: Yes, dear. (VERA *takes the sidecar and pours it straight down.*) Do the Jane Cowl routine. You know, conservative dress, Madonna-like hairdo.

AUNTIE MAME: Madonna-like hairdo. That's it. A switch. A switch.

VERA: Have you got one?

AUNTIE MAME (*going to drawer*): Dozens. (*She pulls out an entire spectrum of switches.*)

VERA: My God, don't you ever throw anything away?

AUNTIE MAME: Who knows when I may go back to one of these colors?

VERA: If you kept your hair natural the way I do, you wouldn't need—

AUNTIE MAME: If I kept my hair natural the way you do, I'd be bald. Pick out the one nearest to mine.

VERA (*picking out the black one and tossing it on the bed*): Try this. And you need a dress—like the one I wore when I played Lady Esme in *Summer Folly*. (MAME *emerges from the closet holding up a striking new gown.*) Oh, that's stunning.

AUNTIE MAME: Isn't it? It's my new Maggie Rouf. But I've never had it on yet. And I'll be damned if I'll put five hundred dollars on my back for that awful man. (*An idea.*) A suit! A suit! That'll do. (*Picks up the switch.*) Help me braid this switch so it looks like a halo.

VERA (*protesting*): I've got to get over to the Guild!

AUNTIE MAME: Vera, you can't desert me!

(VERA *helps* MAME *reluctantly.*)

VERA: *You* should be helping *me.* Do you want me to *lose* this part? (VERA *is braiding* MAME's *switch furiously, then drops it.* MAME *puts one end of the switch in her mouth and braids it herself.*) It's this lovely, lovely play where everybody thinks out loud and it runs four and a half hours. It's called *Strange*—(*She can't remember the title, and gropes for it.*) *Strange Inter—Inter—Inter——*

AUNTIE MAME (*helpfully*): *Course?*

VERA: For God's sake, no. They're opening in Boston. I do hope Lawrence and Terry don't think I'm too British for the part. They'll probably give it to that Lynn what's-her-name.

AUNTIE MAME: Ouch! (*The door buzzer rings.*) Not already! (*Calls.*) Ito, Norah—answer the door!

VERA: I've got to get out before he gets in!

AUNTIE MAME: Well, I can't leave him standing in the foyer like a Fuller Brush man.

VERA: What do you want me to do, fly out the chimney?

MAME: Oh, Vera, for heaven's sake—

VERA (*grandly*): You can't expect me to appear before my public looking as if I'd been slept in!

AUNTIE MAME: Really, Vera —one banker doesn't make a matinee. (*Pinning the braid hastily.*) All right. Wait up here, I'll get rid of him in five minutes—I promise. (*The door buzzer sounds again.* AUNTIE MAME *starts toward the door and the braid topples off.*)

VERA (*simultaneously*): Mame, you just don't understand the responsibility of being in the public eye!

AUNTIE MAME (*exasperated*): Patrick, go downstairs and make Mr. Babcock feel right at home, just like Auntie Mame has taught you.

YOUNG PAT (*going out*): Sure, Auntie Mame.

VERA: But the Theatre Guild—

AUNTIE MAME (*struggling to get the switch anchored*): What am I going to do with this *goddamned halo???????!*

The lighting cross-fades to the foyer. MR. BABCOCK *is punching the door buzzer a little irritably. He is conservative to the very inlays of his molars, with all the personality of a steamroller wearing a vest.* ITO *scurries to the door, carrying a feminine nightgown on a hanger. He opens the door.*

ITO: You want?

BABCOCK: Babcock is the name. Miss Dennis is expecting me.

ITO: Okay. You come in. (*As* BABCOCK *comes in, the lighting rises full on the living room.*) I take coat. (ITO *starts to help* BABCOCK *off with his coat, but cannot manage it while carrying the nightgown. He gives the nightgown to* BABCOCK *who holds it awkwardly.* ITO *starts off with* BABCOCK'S *coat and muffler, leaving the banker holding the nightgown.*) You sit.

BABCOCK: Say—

(ITO *takes the nightgown from the slightly ruffled* BABCOCK, *and scampers off giggling.*

YOUNG PAT *comes down the stairs from* AUNTIE MAME'S *bedroom and greets* MR. BABCOCK *with unaffected composure.*)

YOUNG PAT: Mr. Babcock?

BABCOCK: That's right, Sonny.

YOUNG PAT: We've been expecting you. (*He offers his hand.*) My name is Patrick Dennis.

BABCOCK (*shaking the boy's hand*): Fine, fine.

YOUNG PAT: Please sit down, Mr. Babcock. My Auntie Mame will be right down. She's having trouble with her halo. (*Recovers.*) She'll be right down.

BABCOCK: Fine, fine. (*They look at each other, realizing they have absolutely nothing to communicate.*) Well, you look like a bully little chap. Yes, sir, a bully little chap.

YOUNG PAT: You look very bully, too, Mr. Babcock.

BABCOCK (*clears his throat*): Yes. Well, you seem to be taking all this like a regular little soldier. Oh, say, I have a boy just about your age up in Darien. We'll have you up soon, and Junior can show you his cigar-band collection.

YOUNG PAT (*politely*): That would be swell. (BABCOCK *slaps his knees and rises impatiently.*) Would you care for a martini, Mr. Babcock?

BABCOCK: No, thank you. (*He breaks off, startled, as he sees the hara-kiri painting.*) Maybe you'd better order me one, Sonny.

YOUNG PAT: Dry or extra dry? (BABCOCK *is about to reply, but stops open-mouthed to watch* YOUNG PAT *as he takes down a Martini glass with great finesse, breathes in it, and dries it snappily with a cocktail towel. The boy holds the glass up to the light and squints through it approvingly.*) Please sit down. (BABCOCK's *mouth has sprung open, and apparently he's not going to reply.*) I'll make 'em like I do for Mr. Woollcott. (*From an ice bucket, he drops some cubes into a pitcher; then he pours in a great quantity of gin and stirs.*) Stir— never shake. Bruises the gin. (BABCOCK *nods mechanically.* YOUNG PAT *uncorks the vermouth, pours a smidgeon into the glass, swills it around by rotating the stem, then empties it completely. He fills the glass from the pitcher.*) Would you care for an olive? Auntie Mame says olives take up too much room in such a little glass.

(BABCOCK *shakes his head, his jowls flapping, and takes the glass. The banker takes one sip, then turns to see* AUNTIE MAME *coming down the stairs demurely—complete with braided coronet and all the aplomb of a Scarsdale matron being played by Jane Cowl. She blanches at* YOUNG PAT'S *alcoholic gambit, but makes a lightning recovery.*)

AUNTIE MAME (*grandly*): Why, Mr. Babcock, what an honor it is to have you in our little home. (*She draws him aside, confidentially.*) Though I wonder if it makes the best first impression on a sensitive young mind to see you drinking during business hours.

BABCOCK (*floundering indignantly*): But—but *he*—

AUNTIE MAME (*patting his arm reassuringly*): Don't you

worry, I won't breathe a word to the Knickerbocker Bank.

(BABCOCK *puts down the drink and tries to slide it out of sight, behind him. He can't quite figure out how he has been put on the defensive.*)

BABCOCK: Now, just a minute. Where did that youngster learn to mix a—

AUNTIE MAME (*with dignified hauteur*): Mr. Babcock. Knowledge is power!

(*This stops him.*)

BABCOCK (*clears his throat*): That, Miss Dennis, is exactly what I am here for. To discuss this youngster's education. His *proper* education.

AUNTIE MAME (*offering a dish*): Nuts?

BABCOCK: No, thank you.

AUNTIE MAME: *Do* sit down, Mr. Babcock.

(*They do. MR. BABCOCK finds himself uncomfortably close to the floor on the Japanese settee. AUNTIE MAME sits opposite him, and YOUNG PAT sits on the ottoman between them. He looks back and forth from one speaker to the other as his fate is being decided.*)

BABCOCK (*very businesslike*): Now. All the money this little fella's Dad left him is in good, steady bonds. So he never has to worry where his next meal is coming from. Unless—um—the Bolshevikis take over the government. Or the Democrats get back in.

AUNTIE MAME: Jelly beans?

BABCOCK (*taking one*): Now I'm sure you agree that it's

high time this little shaver was enrolled in some institution of learning.

YOUNG PAT (*brightly*): Oh, I'm already—

AUNTIE MAME: Now, now. Let Mr. Babcock talk, dear.

BABCOCK: Now. I've gone to, uh, some pains to, uh, gather information on a number of the better boys' schools in town.

AUNTIE MAME: Personally, I prefer coeducational schools.

BABCOCK (*shocked*): What do you mean?

YOUNG PAT (*helpfully*): Coeducational means when boys and girls go—

BABCOCK: I know. I know. (*Clears his throat.*) First on my list is the Buckley School, which is known to be splendid.

AUNTIE MAME: Have you considered a school down in the Village run by a Mr. Ralph Devine? It's wonderfully progressive and—

BABCOCK (*holding up a hand as if directing rush-hour traffic*): Your late brother was very specific in his will. He said *conservative* schooling. (*Consulting his list.*) Now, the Browning School gives a boy the basics. Three years of Latin—

(*While* BABCOCK *is speaking,* VERA *appears at the top of the stairs behind him. She gesticulates vigorously to* MAME, *who is facing her.* BABCOCK *looks up.*)

AUNTIE MAME (*covering*): That's enough candy, dear. Not you, Mr. Babcock. Have as much as you like. (*Quickly.*) Have you thought of the Dalton School? It's right up—

BABCOCK: No, no. That one is a *li*ttle too experimental. (*He digs out several pamphlets.*) We must choose a school that is both exclusive and restricted.

AUNTIE MAME (*gritting her teeth*): Exclusively *what* and restricted to *whom?*

BABCOCK: Want to keep the riffraff out of this lad's life—

(MAME *rises, about to explode.*)

AUNTIE MAME: Mr. Babbitt—

BABCOCK: Bab*cock.*

AUNTIE MAME: Yes. Uh—exactly who decides which is riff and which is raff?

BABCOCK: Now, Miss Dennis, unless we can agree on some proper school here in Manhattan, we shall have to consider an institution such as *my* alma mater, St. Boniface, up in Massachusetts.

AUNTIE MAME: No, no, that's too far away! Have you thought of the Ethical Culture School—that's just across town?

BABCOCK: I'd like to keep that West-side influence out of the boy's life as much as possible.

(AUNTIE MAME *stands, icily, indicating that the interview is over.*)

AUNTIE MAME: It was very good of you to come, Mr. Babcock.

BABCOCK: But we haven't arrived at any conclusions.

AUNTIE MAME: Haven't we?

BABCOCK: Well, what school is it going to be?

AUNTIE MAME: You name the school of your choice, and Patrick and I will know exactly what to do.

BABCOCK (*strongly*): I'd say Buckley.

AUNTIE MAME: Then *bully* for Buckley.

BABCOCK: Well—(*This was easier than he thought it would be.*) For a minute there, I thought we were going to have a little friction. (*He chortles.*) But I'm glad to see you're actually a fine, sensible woman. I'll make out a check to the Buckley School and you can take him down and register him.

AUNTIE MAME (*sweetly*): Whatever you say. Well, it's so nice of you to—

(VERA, *with a scarf tied around her head and a peasant babushka, plods across the room. She is wearing* MAME'S *new Maggie Rouf and dragging* MAME'S *best mink on the floor behind her.*)

VERA (*in a thick accent*): Floor all scrubbed, *Fraulein* Dennis. Clean yoost like in old country. I go now, get lamb chops, two bottles milk for boy.

AUNTIE MAME (*between her teeth*): Pick up my coat.

YOUNG PAT: Good-by, Auntie Vera.

VERA (*back in her own voice*): 'By, kid.

(*There is a big take from the already bewildered* BAB-COCK *as the lights fade.*)

The panels of the living room have been switched and the furnishings have been redressed, as much as time will allow. The wallpaper is now modern.

The phone rings. The PAPERHANGER *is coming down his ladder, looks around at his handiwork, shakes his head.* ITO *enters from the foyer, carrying a chart.*

PAPERHANGER: Phone's ringin'.

(*He goes out.* ITO *puts down the chart, facing upstage, and picks up the phone.*)

ITO (*into phone*): Missy Dennis residence. Stockbroker? Missy Dennis not here, you call back next month sometime. (*He listens.*) Missy Dennis say anybody who call servant dirty bastard is dirty bastard. (*He puts down the phone, smiling happily.*)

(NORAH *enters in a hat and coat, her arms full of groceries.*)

NORAH (*to* ITO): Now, where've *you* been?

ITO: Missy Dennis send me 'cross ocean. Staten Island. Bring back body.

NORAH: What body?

ITO: For boy.

NORAH (*reading cover on chart*): "The Physiological Anatomical Medical Supply Company." What in the name of St. Bridget is it?

ITO: Missy say boy gotta know inside like outside. (*He flips over the cover, revealing a skeleton.*)

NORAH: Oh, the poor man. Nothin' but a liver, God rest his soul. (*She crosses herself.*)

ITO (*starting upstairs with chart*): Missy say put in boy's room.

NORAH: I dare ya. There's not an inch of space left up there.

ITO: I make space. I put white mice your room. (*He giggles.*)

NORAH (*as she goes into kitchen*): Put 'em in your own pagoda, ya heathen!

(AUNTIE MAME *and* LINDSAY *come in the foyer. They are loaded down with packages and boxes.* AUNTIE MAME *is aglow with excitement and decked out in furs, but* LINDSAY *is getting a little tired of this maternal bit. They come into the apartment.*)

AUNTIE MAME: What a day! What a lovely, lovely day!

LINDSAY: What a day is right. On our feet for five hours— no lunch. Why don't they put a bar in F.A.O. Schwartz? I haven't even had a chance to call my office. I might have been bought out by Knopf.

AUNTIE MAME: Stop complaining, Lindsay. Fix yourself a drink. And then we can open the parcels. I can't wait to see Patrick's face when he sees all these lovely things.

LINDSAY: Mame! When are we going to have a day, an hour, a minute—some time to ourselves?

AUNTIE MAME: Time! Lindsay, don't you realize I've had to make up for Patrick's ten neglected years in a matter of months. (*Picking up a brightly colored book.*) Dr. Gesell says it's practically an impossibility.

LINDSAY: Does Dr. Gesell also happen to mention that what a child needs is a father?

AUNTIE MAME: Now, Lindsay—

LINDSAY (*pressing on*): You know there are a lot of women in this town who think I'm a reasonably good catch. I'm reasonably successful; you've admitted yourself that I'm reasonably attractive, I'm reasonably—

AUNTIE MAME: Oh, Lindsay, that's the trouble. You're "reasonably" everything. You're reasonably in love with me, and we'd be reasonably happy. But that's not enough. Besides, how can I be a wife? I'm too busy being a mother.

(*The doorbell buzzes.*)

LINDSAY: There was Coué, Dada, Nature Foods, modern dance—

AUNTIE MAME: Oh, you think Patrick is a *phase*—

LINDSAY: Well, frankly, I do.

(BABCOCK *bursts in.*)

BABCOCK: Where is she? Where is that madwoman? Where is that irresponsible, deceitful Bohemian Delilah?

(LINDSAY *tries to protest throughout the entire following scene—but never succeeds in getting more than a word in edgewise.*)

LINDSAY: Now, just a minute, sir—

AUNTIE MAME (*with a hollow hauteur*): Why, Mr. Babcock, whatever do you mean?

BABCOCK: You know damned well what I mean. Why, you're no more fit to raise a child than Jezebel!

(AUNTIE MAME, *concerned, rushes forward.*)

AUNTIE MAME: Patrick! Something's happened to my little love!

BABCOCK: You're damned right someth— Come in here, you little heathen! (*He drags the boy into the room.* YOUNG PAT *huddles in an overcoat.*)

AUNTIE MAME: Patrick—what's wrong?

(*Before the boy can answer,* BABCOCK *thunders on.*)

PATRICK: Well, he came over to my school—

BABCOCK: I'll tell you what's wrong. I was doing my conscientious duty. I dropped by the Buckley School to check on the kid's academic standing. And what did I find? He isn't even registered. Never has been. So I've been hunting in every low, half-baked school for the feeble-minded in this town. And finally I found him —in the lowest of them all.

AUNTIE MAME: Mr. Devine is a progressive educator. He

uses the same theory Bertrand Russell does in England—

BABCOCK: I walk into that so-called "institution of learning"—and what do I find? A whole schoolroom of 'em —boys, girls, teachers—romping around, stark naked! Bare as the day they were born!

AUNTIE MAME: I can assure you that the students under Mr. Devine's care were engaged in healthful, broadening pursuits.

BABCOCK: Broadening! (*Turns to* YOUNG PAT.) Show 'em what you were doing when I broke into the place. Go ahead—show 'em!

YOUNG PAT: We were just playing fish families.

BABCOCK: "Fish families!"

YOUNG PAT: It's part of constructive play.

BABCOCK: Listen to this.

AUNTIE MAME: Show me, darling.

YOUNG PAT: Well, we do it just after Yogurt Time. Mrs. Devine and all the girls crouch down on the floor under the sun lamps—and they pretend to be lady-fishes, depositing their eggs in the sand. Then Mr. Devine and all the boys do what gentlemen fish do.

AUNTIE MAME: What could be more wholesome or natural?

BABCOCK: Natural! It might be natural for a sardine! (*To* LINDSAY.) Would you put a boy of yours in a school like that?

AUNTIE MAME: Mr. Babcock. I consider your behavior most undignified.

BABCOCK: Undignified! At least I'm wearing a vest.

AUNTIE MAME: Making a scene. Causing what might well be a traumatic experience for this child.

BABCOCK (*holding up a hand*): Look, I know how you can twist things around. So I'm getting out of this combination nudist camp-opium den before you make *me* look like the vice-president in charge of free love!

AUNTIE MAME (*righteously covering* PAT'S *ears*): Mr. Babcock. Not in front of the B-O-Y!

(BABCOCK *goes toward the exit, turns threateningly.*) *continue here*

BABCOCK: Tomorrow morning, I, me, *personally*—I'm taking this kid off to boarding school myself. I'm placing him in St. Boniface Academy and he's going to stay there. The only time you'll get your depraved hands on him is Christmas and summer, and I wish to God there was some way to prevent that.

YOUNG PAT (*running to* AUNTIE MAME): Auntie Mame. Do I have to? Do I?

AUNTIE MAME (*frantically*): Please, Mr. Babcock—I'll do whatever you say. If you'll only let the child stay near me.

BABCOCK: Not on your life! He goes, and he goes tomorrow.

LINDSAY: Now let's be reasonable about this—

BABCOCK: I'm going to turn this kid into a decent, God-fearing Christian if I have to break every bone in his body.

AUNTIE MAME: If you'll give me another chance—

BABCOCK: I wouldn't give you the time of day, after the dirty doublecross you pulled on me.

AUNTIE MAME (*pleading in real desperation*): Mr. Babcock, he's all I have, he's my life.

BABCOCK: You have him ready by eight o'clock *sharp*. And, kid, you'd better be wearing knickers! (*He exits.*)

YOUNG PAT: I want to stay with you, Auntie Mame. I don't want to go to that old St. Bony Face.

AUNTIE MAME: Hush, my little love. I'm sure St. Boniface is really very nice. Now, go upstairs and get ready for dinner, and we'll talk about it later. (*She watches as* PAT *climbs the stairs.*) Lindsay, Lindsay. What am I going to do?

LINDSAY (*honestly concerned*): Don't worry, Mame. I'll help you. I'll get the kid back some way.

AUNTIE MAME (*crying*): I just don't think I can bear it. I just don't—

LINDSAY: Mame, I've never seen you cry before . . . (LINDSAY *tries to comfort her. The doorbell jabs insistently, and we hear the strident voice of* VERA *in the outside hall.*)

VERA (*from off*): Mame, are you in there?

AUNTIE MAME: Oh, I just couldn't take anything else today!

VERA: It's urgent, it's vital, it's *dire!* (*She hurries on.*) Have you talked to your stockbroker? (*She looks at the unhappy* MAME.) Yes. I can see you have.

LINDSAY: What about her stockbroker?

VERA: Don't you know? He's called me half a dozen times, trying to locate both of you.

LINDSAY (*paling slightly*): What happened?

VERA: Oh, nothing—except that nothing's worth anything any more!

(*Phone rings.*)

LINDSAY: Don't you worry, Mame. I'm sure this is only something temporary. It can't possibly affect people like you and me—who have a lot of solid stuff like Bank of the United States.

(ITO *scampers to answer the phone.*)

ITO (*he covers the mouthpiece, then speaks blandly to* AUNTIE MAME): Missy Dennis. Stockbroker want to say hello before he jump out of window.

(LINDSAY *grabs phone.*)

LINDSAY (*into phone*): How bad is it, Arthur? (*The blood drains from his face.*) Everything? (*He can hardly say it.*) Atwater-Kent, too???????? (*Slowly he puts down the telephone, stunned.*) Mame, I'm afraid you're wiped out. We *all* are.

VERA (*philosophically*): And everybody said I was such a fool, spending all my money at Tiffany's.

AUNTIE MAME: Who gives a damn about money? I've lost my child.

VERA: What?

LINDSAY: Patrick's trustee is sending him away to school.

VERA: Oh, Mame, darling—I know how you must feel.

AUNTIE MAME: Do you?

VERA: Well, not exactly, of course. I've never *had* a child. But, after all, I'm an actress, I can imagine. (*Abruptly, businesslike*.) Now look—I've got everything worked out for you—I've got the perfect solution for all your problems. I'm going to tell Brock he simply *has* to give you a part in my new play. It opens Thanksgiving in New Haven.

AUNTIE MAME: No, thanks, Vera, I don't want your charity, I don't want anything but—

VERA: No, no, darling! It isn't charity, I want you in it. Besides, Patrick's trustee is sure to let Patrick come back when he finds out you've settled down into something steady like acting.

AUNTIE MAME: Do you really think so, Vera?

VERA: Oh, I know he would. Don't you agree, Lindsay?

LINDSAY: Well—

AUNTIE MAME: Oh, but you're so right, Vera. And if he didn't, I'd be earning the money to fight him. About five hundred dollars a week to start, don't you think? And then there'll be a raise—

VERA: Mame, it'll only be a bit—at the end of the last act. (*Persuasively*.) But it'll be like old times! Think of the fun we had trouping together in *Chu-Chin-Chow*.

AUNTIE MAME: I accept, I accept. Vera, your heart is from Tiffany's, too. Oh, I can't wait to hear the overture!

VERA: Mame—this is a drama. Serious drama. I play the part of a Balkan princess who—

MAME (*to* LINDSAY): I was in the front line of the chorus and Vera was behind me.

VERA: Behind you! If I'd been behind you, I'd have kicked you in the behind, you.

AUNTIE MAME (*sings illustratively*): "I'm a Chu-Chu girl
from Chu-Chin-Chow
        And how!" (*Clicks tongue.*)
        "And how!" (*Clicks tongue.*)

VERA (*pushes* MAME *into the back row*): "I'd love to chin
and chew with you."

AUNTIE MAME (*with elaborate gestures*): "And turn the
skies to blue with you."

VERA (*showing her how it was really done*): "And turn the
skies to blue with you."

AUNTIE MAME: That's it!

BOTH (*harmonizing*): "And twenty-three skidoo with you!
Chee-Chee!   Choo-Choo!   Chow-Chow!"   (*Click
tongues.*) "And how!" (*Click tongues.*)

(*Hilariously, they fall into each other's arms. Merci-
fully the lights fade on the two Sing-Sing Girls.*)

scene 8

*The stage of the Shubert Theatre, reverse angle. In
the darkness, we hear the* STAGE MANAGER'S *voice.*

STAGE MANAGER: Set up for Act Three, Scene Two. And
quiet on stage. There are still critics out there—I
hope.

MAID: I can't find my feather duster.

STAGE MANAGER: Props! Get 'em their feather dusters.
Lemme have a worklight, Bob. (*The worklight comes
on.*) Bring in the finale drop.

(*The* THEATER MANAGER *rushes backstage. He is a
splenetic man with glasses and a cigar, bred by the
Shuberts.*)

THEATER MANAGER (*pointing upstage to the theater audience behind the house curtain*): Look, half the audience out there has gone home, and the other half has
gone to sleep. Does this play ever *end????*

STAGE MANAGER: We're almost set, Mr. Unger.

(*The* ASSISTANT STAGE MANAGER *comes out with a prop-bench.*)

ASSISTANT STAGE MANAGER: Miss Dennis ain't ready.

THEATER MANAGER: Who the hell is Miss Dennis?

STAGE MANAGER: She plays Lady Iris.

THEATER MANAGER: That's a two-line bit.

STAGE MANAGER: Shh—!

ASSISTANT STAGE MANAGER (*starting off*): She wants more time to arrange her accessories.

STAGE MANAGER (*exploding*): She's had two and a half acts to arrange her damned accessories.

THEATER MANAGER: Get that curtain up—and if that Dennis dame ain't ready—(*He clamps the cigar in his teeth.*)—I'll play Lady Iris.

STAGE MANAGER: Lights. Kill the worklight. Take it up, Bob.

(*The audience for this play-within-a-play is presumed to be at extreme upstage.*

The worklight goes off. The curtain, upstage, rises, and we see footlights and balcony rails shining directly into our faces. The business of the play, therefore, is directed upstage; but the asides in the following are given downstage, to the actual theater audience.

The MAID *and* BUTLER *dust furiously. Everything the* BUTLER *dusts, the* MAID *dusts again immediately afterward.*)

MAID: What do you suppose is happening now, Meadows, in the conservatory?

BUTLER: It is all over, Perkins. It is done with! We have lost the master—and, worst than that, the master has lost himself.

MAID: But love burns bright in this house tonight, Meadows!

BUTLER: And we shall all be consumed in the flames!

MAID: Don't be ridiculous, Meadows. Tonight we are living a legend. There is a *princess* beneath this roof, and every room vibrates with the fragrance of this fragile royal flower!

BUTLER: And our master is drugged by the heady perfume.

MAID (*quickly, resuming her dusting*): Hush, Meadows. They are coming now!

(*The* MAID *and* BUTLER *scurry off. From the opposite side,* VERA *and her leading man enter dramatically.* VERA *is svelte and statuesque, and her leading man is more of a matinee idol than is absolutely necessary. He always seems about to speak, but never manages to get a line out—*VERA *has seen to that; she also does a polished job of upstaging the poor guy.*)

VERA: But, Rrrreginald, tew dew sech a thing—tew desh oaf tewgethaw lake thisss—would be med; quate enchantingly med. (AUNTIE MAME *comes into the wings, in flaming red.* NORAH *is helping her as she does last-minute primping. On her wrists are clanging bell bracelets.*) Ooooooooh, Lord Dudley. Your flahterry is enough to turn a young girl's head! (*There is the tinkling of bells.* VERA *touches her coiffure and begins*

again.) Naow, Rreginald, it would be medness. Ay be-
lung tew one wuld, yew tew anothah. It's bettah thet
we paht now; now whale we cheddish this ecstasy
we've known. (VERA *moves regally toward the wings,
then speaking away from her audience, but so we can
hear clearly, she drops all affectation and speaks in
good clear Pittsburgh.*) What the hell have you got
back there—reindeer? (*She wheels upstage toward her
own audience and instantaneously resumes her May-
fair elegance.*) This is gudbay, Rreginald. Ay heah the
othahs coming.

(THE OTHERS *sweep on, led by* AUNTIE MAME *on the
arm of an embarrassed stage* LORD DUDLEY. *Around her
wrists are the bracelets we have seen—and heard—
before: fashioned from large silver Siamese temple
bells. With every gesture, she drowns out the dialogue.*

VERA *glares at her with all the loving kindness of the
Apache Kid on the warpath.*)

AUNTIE MAME (*as she enters; with an uninhibited stage
laugh*): Ooooooh, no mahr champagne, Lord Dudleh,
or I shall forget myself altogethah! (*She makes a
sweeping gesture and the bells clang like New Year's
Eve.*)

VERA (*frigidly poking* MAME *in the back with her elbow*):
Ay've sumthing tew tale yew ull. Ay'm nut gaowing
to meddy Rrrreginald after ull. May place is at haome
with Prince Alexiss. Ay must gaow beck—beck to *may*
wuld. (REGINALD *looks crushed.* AUNTIE MAME, *on a*

sudden Stanislavsky impulse, pats his arm comfortingly. The effect is as subtle as the passing of a fire engine. REGINALD *steps out of reach.* VERA *turns to* AUNTIE MAME, *with a look that would paralyze the average Bengal tiger.*) Lady Irrriss. Would yew be gude enough to rrring for my wrrrap!

AUNTIE MAME: Certainly, Princess. (*She curtsies deeply; the bells peal deafeningly. A* FOOTMAN *hands* AUNTIE MAME *the wrap, folded. It is a voluminous chinchilla. As* AUNTIE MAME *advances to* VERA, VERA *turns toward us and mutters menacingly.*)

VERA: And get rid of those goddam cowbells! (*Flustered,* AUNTIE MAME *tries to muffle the bells in the coat as* VERA *turns with a gracious wave toward her audience.*)

AUNTIE MAME: Do let me help you, Princess. (*She puts the* cape over VERA'S *shoulders upside down, the hem at her neck, the collar sweeping the floor.*)

VERA: Thenk yew, Lady Iris. (*An awful look comes over her face as she realizes the cape is upside down. She points down her back to the collar.* AUNTIE MAME *engages in a brief but unsuccessful battle with the chinchilla.* VERA *decides to get off, and quick.*) Gudbay, gudbay. I shell always feel a deep attachment for you ull! (*As* VERA *sweeps off,* AUNTIE MAME'S *outstretched hand mysteriously remains connected to the small of* VERA'S *back, so that she is tugged along toward the exit. The bells keep clanging.* VERA *grunts, over her shoulder.*) Let go. For God's sake, *let go!*

AUNTIE MAME (*helplessly wailing*): I can't let go. I'm caught. *I'm stuck!*

(There is some less-than-amiable thrashing as the two women try to disentangle themselves.)

STAGE MANAGER'S VOICE *(off, frantic)*: Curtain! Bring down the curtain! *(There is the anaesthetic lowering of velour, cutting off the ribald laughter and catcalls.)* Places for curtain calls!

(The ACTORS make a formal line facing upstage, but AUNTIE MAME is still enmeshed with VERA.)

VERA: You amateur!

(The curtain rises, and ALL bow graciously to the audience upstage. The curtain comes down.)

AUNTIE MAME *(miserable)*: I was only trying—
VERA: Ruining my beautiful play with your goddam Swiss bell-ringing act!
AUNTIE MAME: But, Vera, they're the only bracelets I have left—

(The curtain goes up again for a second curtain time. More bows. VERA flings off the encumbrance of the chinchilla and AUNTIE MAME. She does this with such violence that AUNTIE MAME is catapulted forward into what seems to be a solo curtain call. The applause is thunderous.)

VERA: That's enough!

(The curtain falls again. The STAGE MANAGER comes on, wild-eyed.)

STAGE MANAGER: That's enough! Strike the set! Worklight!

VERA (*wheeling on* MAME): Why did you do this to me? Why?

AUNTIE MAME (*honestly distraught*): I was only trying to make something out of Lady Iris—give her some character . . .

VERA: You scene-stealing society bitch! (*Turns her back on* AUNTIE MAME.) Oh, God. And there were *critics* out there. We're ruined. We're all ruined. (*As she goes off.*) Ruined. Ruined.

(*She's gone. The others in the cast avoid* AUNTIE MAME *as if she had a touch of leprosy.*)

AUNTIE MAME: I was only trying to—I was only—

(*They're all gone now—and just the bare worklights and a box remain on the empty stage.*

AUNTIE MAME *sinks down, alone and dismal.*

YOUNG PAT *comes hesitantly toward* AUNTIE MAME, *pausing at the edge of the circle of light.*)

YOUNG PAT: I thought you were very good, Auntie Mame. Everybody noticed you.

AUNTIE MAME: Oh, my little love. How did you get to New Haven?

YOUNG PAT: Ito brought me up.

AUNTIE MAME: But how could he drive you up when I've already sold the car?

YOUNG PAT (*brightly*): Oh, he didn't drive; we hitchhiked!

AUNTIE MAME: But Mr. Babcock thinks you're in that horrible school—

YOUNG PAT (*patting her shoulder*): It's all right, Auntie Mame. It's Thanksgiving vacation.

AUNTIE MAME (*looking around the stage forlornly*): Is it?

(*He comes to her and puts his arm around her tenderly.*)

YOUNG PAT: Can I be your escort? Can I take you back to your hotel?

AUNTIE MAME (*tears in her eyes*): You can take me all the way back to New York. Oh, Patrick, are you ashamed of your Auntie Mame?

YOUNG PAT: I'm *proud* of you. Nobody liked the stinky old play at all until you came in. (YOUNG PAT *kisses her lightly on the cheek. Then he takes a step back, bows slightly from the waist, offering his arm.*) Lady Iris?

(*She smiles in spite of her dejection, rises, takes his arm.*)

AUNTIE MAME: Chahmed, Lord Dudley!

(*She makes an Edwardian gesture. They start off together, and she hugs him close as the lights fade.*)

Telephone switchboard. Buzzing in darkness. We see
AUNTIE MAME *wrestling with the plugs. Several are*
already in place.

AUNTIE MAME: Widdicombe, Gutterman, Applewhite,
Bibberman, and Black—good morning. One moment,
I'll connect you with Mr. Gutterman. (*She plugs.*)
Widdicombe, Gutterman, Applewhite, Bibberman,
and Black, good—Yes, Mr. Bibberman, I'll get you
Mr. Applewhite. (*She crosses two plugs, one from each
board to the other.*) Widdicombe, Gutterman, Applewhite, Bibberman, and Black. Good morning. Long
Distance—(*She plugs.*) Mr. Widdicombe, I have your
San Francisco call. (*She plugs.*) Yes, Mr. Bibberman.
(*Innocently.*) Oh, did I give you Mr. Gutterman instead of Mr. Applewhite? I'm sorry, Mr. Bibber-
combe—uh, Bibbebib. (*She pulls down a plug from
one side and starts to put it in the other side. But
there is already a plug in the hole she wants to put it
in. She pulls down the offending plug from the hole*

*with her other hand and holds it up, addressing it as
if it were a person.)* Mr. Applewhite, what were you
doing in that hole with Mr. Gutterman? *(She now has
two plugs, one in each hand. Forgetting where they
are supposed to go, she thrusts one plug in her bodice
to free her hand for another call. She puts up another
plug.)* Mr. Widdicombe, I'll try to reconnect you with
San Francisco. Now, let me see . . . *(She starts re-
arranging the plugs at random, sticking one plug in
her mouth.)* Mr. Bibberbip is in there and Mr. Gut-
terwipe is talking to—And where's Mr. Applewhite?
*(The board is going crazy now. She is plugging and
unplugging frantically now. Buzz.)* Oh, there you
are, Mr. Applewhite. Yes, sir. *(She dials.)* Eldorado
five—two one two one. Yes, sir. Hold on, Mr. Widde-
combe. I'll find San Francisco. *(Buzz.)* Widdicombe,
Gutterman, Applewhite. Oh! Supervisor? I did? *(She
pushes a key.)* I'm afraid you gave me a wrong number, sir. There is *no* Applewhite five, Mr. Eldorado.
(The lights fade as the frantic buzzing continues.) I
don't know what I did with San Francisco.

(The lights are out.)

A roller skate counter at Macy's. "Silent Night" is playing peacefully against the cacophony of people assailing the roller skate counter. But there is no clerk behind the counter.

SHOPPER (*calling angrily*): Floorwalker! Do I have to wait until New Year's to straighten out these roller skates?

(MR. LOOMIS, *a carnation wearing a man, is trying to mollify the customers.*)

MR. LOOMIS: If you'll just be patient, Madame, I'm certain our roller skate lady will be here momentarily. (*Raising his voice, sing song, to "Silent Night."*) Roller skate lady. Where is the roller skate lady?

SHOPPER: Your stupid clerk sent me two left roller skates. Does Macy's think my kid has two left feet—is that what you think?

MR. LOOMIS: Perhaps we'd better take this up with the Complaint Department. If you'll just step this way, Madame. (*The* SHOPPER *storms off with* MR. LOOMIS.) Christmas. God deliver us.

(AUNTIE MAME *enters with a* WOMAN. MAME *is carry-ing a Tinker-Toy box and a sales book.*)

WOMAN: Clerk, clerk. Am I ever going to get out of here? All I want are these roller skates.

AUNTIE MAME: I don't know how I got over there in Tinker Toys. (*Calling rather plaintively.*) Mr. Loomis? Would you help me with this sales slip, please? (MAME *opens the sales book. This is the most bedrag-gled sales book in the history of retail selling. Carbons, tissues spill out in hectic disarray.* MAME *turns back to her customer.*) Oh, Mrs. Jennings, why don't you let me send these to you C.O.D.? Then you won't have to pay any money at all!

WOMAN: Well, I would eventually—

AUNTIE MAME: Don't you worry your head about it, Mrs. Jennings. I'll take care of everything. (*Up.*) Never mind, Mr. Loomis. (*She scribbles a slip.*)

WOMAN: Now, just a minute—

AUNTIE MAME: Here's your slip now. See? You don't even have any bundles to carry. (*The* WOMAN *goes off.*) Oh, I just love C.O.D.

(*During the above, a fine-looking Southern gentle-man comes on. This is a hell of a guy; you can tell it from the genuineness of his smile. He's rosy-cheeked, with steel-gray hair. His camel's-hair coat and Cava-naugh hat indicate a cozy opulence. This is* BEAURE-GARD JACKSON PICKETT BURNSIDE. AUNTIE MAME *turns to him. Reflexively, her eyelids flutter slightly.*)

BEAU (*in a deep musical Southern drawl*): Ma'am, would

you be good enough to assist me in ordering twenty-four pairs of those fine-looking roller skates?

AUNTIE MAME (*taken aback*): Twenty-four! My, what a proud father you must be!

BEAU (*chortles*): Oh, they're not my children, ma'am; I'm a single gentleman. But a lot of little tykes at the Oglethorpe Orphanage—just outside of Savannah—are gonna pop their eyes out when this package arrives. (*He reaches in his pocket for a roll of bills that would choke a mastodon.*) Now, how much does that come to, little lady?

(AUNTIE MAME, *fumbling with the sales book, looks at the roll of bills dismayed.*)

AUNTIE MAME: You want to pay? *Cash?*

BEAU: Oglethorpe Orphanage. R.F.D. 2, Savannah, Georgia.

(AUNTIE MAME *starts to write, then stops and looks round like a trapped animal.*)

AUNTIE MAME: Are you sure you wouldn't rather have these go C.O.D.?

BEAU (*laughs heartily*): Now, what would those little nippers think if their Uncle Beau sent 'em a Christmas present *co*-llect on *de*-livery.

AUNTIE MAME: Mr. Loomis—!

BEAU (*he is now most gallant*): If it would be any aid to you, ma'am, I suppose I could *take* the package with me.

AUNTIE MAME: Oh, no. That's worse. (*She looks around as*

if she were admitting former membership in the Communist Party.) You see, I haven't worked here very long. And the only kind of sales slip I know how to make out is C.O.D.

BEAU: Well, now. Maybe I can be of some assistance, little lady. I've got a passing familiarity with *fi*-nancial matters. (*He comes behind the counter and takes the sales book out of her hands and starts to write up the order. This gives* AUNTIE MAME *a chance to size up* BEAU, *with some admiration.*)

AUNTIE MAME: You'd better not come back here.

BEAU: First you gotta get your dupl*icates* and tripl*icates* straightened out, elsewise Mr. Macy won't have any way of knowin' what you sold.

AUNTIE MAME: I never thought of that.

BEAU: First the name—(*Writes.*) Beauregard Jackson Pickett Burnside.

AUNTIE MAME: That's a long name to get on such a little slip.

(BEAU *writes with amazing efficiency, and* AUNTIE MAME *peeks over his shoulder.* MR. LOOMIS *comes on. He rises to his full five feet five.*)

MR. LOOMIS: Miss Dennis, may I inquire what is going on here?

AUNTIE MAME (*floundering*): Well, Mr. Loomis, this nice gentleman simply offered to—

BEAU: This little lady—Miss Dennis, is that your name?— she was having a mite of trouble making out my sales slip for a couple of dozen roller skates—

MR. LOOMIS (*frigidly*): Was there something *unusual* about the order?

AUNTIE MAME: Yes. He wants to pay *cash!*

MR. LOOMIS (*incredulously*): Am I to understand that a Macy employee doesn't know how to make a *cash sale?????*

AUNTIE MAME: I'm a whiz at C.O.D.'s. You can see—

(MR. LOOMIS *seizes the sales book and leafs through it in amazement.*)

MR. LOOMIS: Miss Dennis, this sales book is a shambles. You are obviously incompetent to dispense merchandise. You will report to personnel immediately for your dismissal.

BEAU (*trying to gloss over the matter*): Now, she was just doin' the best she knew how—

MR. LOOMIS: Well, it's not good enough for the R. H. Macy Company! (LOOMIS *starts off, still leafing through the sales book.*) Good heavens, it'll take auditing a week to straighten out this mess.

(BEAU *follows, protesting.*)

BEAU: Now, you listen here to me, sir. I feel entirely responsible for bringing about this unfortunate misunderstandin'.

(AUNTIE MAME *gets her purse from under the counter and starts off in the opposite direction. Thinking of a moneyless Christmas up ahead, she is sad and dispirited. Suddenly she remembers something and calls*

across to BEAU *as he disappears on the tail of* MR.
LOOMIS.)

AUNTIE MAME (*calling*): Don't forget the roller skates for
those little nippers. (*Sniffs, then belligerently.*) Get
'em at Gimbels!!!!!

(*The* SHOPPERS *drift off, and lighting on the Macy
area fades. Behind the crowd* AUNTIE MAME *has slipped
on a somewhat threadbare cloth overcoat. We hear a
legato, disconsolate "Deck the Halls" as a spot follows* MAME, *downhearted and desolate.*)

The Beekman Place apartment lights up softly. Some of the furnishings and expensive hangings are gone. There is a Christmas tree. YOUNG PAT *is just finishing decorating it.*

Moving continuously from the previous scene, AUNTIE MAME *walks into the apartment, stands looking at* YOUNG PAT *and the grubby little tree.*

YOUNG PAT *turns and sees her.*

YOUNG PAT: Auntie Mame! Gee, I didn't expect you home so soon.

AUNTIE MAME: Well, they kinda gave me my Christmas vacation a little bit early. But I'm glad, really. Because now it fits with *your* vacation—and we won't have to miss even a day together.

YOUNG PAT: How do you like the tree? I decorated it myself. Aren't you surprised?

(AUNTIE MAME *sinks down on an ottoman and involuntarily her hand covers her face.*)

AUNTIE MAME: It's beautiful, dear, it's simply beautiful. (*She chokes up.* YOUNG PAT, *fully aware of her low spirits, determines to cheer her up. He reaches behind the tree for an oblong jeweler's package.*)

YOUNG PAT: I'm going to give you your Christmas present right now. You don't even have to wait till Christmas morning. (*He hands it to her.*) Here. Open it.

(*Really speechless,* AUNTIE MAME *unwraps the tissue.*)

AUNTIE MAME: Patrick! Where did you get the money?

YOUNG PAT: Mr. Leavitt at the Pawn Shop gave me a very good price for my microscope and my hockey stick.

AUNTIE MAME: Patrick!

YOUNG PAT: I was getting kinda tired of microbes.

(AUNTIE MAME *opens the package and holds up a rhinestone bracelet in excellent taste. She shakes her head with dazed happiness.*)

AUNTIE MAME: Oh, my.

YOUNG PAT: They're not *quite* diamonds.

AUNTIE MAME: Oh, darling, that's the most beautiful bracelet I've ever owned. (*She kisses him.*)

YOUNG PAT: Wiggle it! (*She does. No sound.*) See. It doesn't make any noise. I told the man you had to have a quiet one—for when you go on the stage again. (*She puts it on. He helps her fasten the clasp.*) And when you wear it with your mink coat—why, nobody will ever know you work at Macy's!

AUNTIE MAME: I've given up Macy's, dear. And my mink coat is down at Mr. Leavitt's with your hockey stick. (AUNTIE MAME *gets up and shakes the depression as if she were discarding a garment. Calling.*) Norah! Ito! If we're going to have Christmas, let's have it all the way around. (*She goes to a drawer and takes out several small boxes.*)

(NORAH *and* ITO *come on,* ITO *drawing on his house coat.*)

ITO: Yes, Missy Dennis?

(AUNTIE MAME *hands each of them a package.*)

AUNTIE MAME: Merry Christmas, everybody.

NORAH: But it isn't until Tuesday, mum.

ITO: Miss Dennis get mixed up with calendar again. Not Christmas yet.

AUNTIE MAME: Well, we *need* it now—so let's go ahead and have it. (*They start to unwrap their packages eagerly.*) I did want to pay you some of your back salary, but—

NORAH: Now, not another word about it, mum. You know we wouldn't think of leavin' you.

ITO (*cheerfully*): No place else get job anyhow. (ITO *lifts out an inexpensive wrist watch.*) Ohhhhh.

AUNTIE MAME: It isn't seventeen jewels, Ito—but I'm not sure that time is worth all that decoration these days.

ITO: Thank you, Missy.

(NORAH *opens a box of perfume, cologne, and bath salts, unscrews and smells each one.*)

NORAH: It's so French-smellin'! I'll be the most aromatic thing on Beekman Place.

(YOUNG PAT *has been wrestling with the suit box. Now*

he has it open and he holds up a pair of long pants.)

YOUNG PAT: Golly! Long pants! At last. (*Eagerly.*) Can I try 'em on, Auntie Mame? Right now?

AUNTIE MAME: Right now.

(YOUNG PAT *dashes upstairs.*

ITO *and* NORAH *exchange glances, then decide to speak.*)

NORAH: Well, we got a little present for you, too, mum—Ito and me. Now I hope you're not gonna be angry for what we done.

(ITO *scampers out, reappearing almost immediately with something behind his back.*)

AUNTIE MAME: Just what is it you have done?

NORAH (*blurts it out*): Well, Ito had a bit of money put by —and so did I—for a rainy day, you might say. But we both figgered it couldn't get much wetter than it is right now.

ITO: We pay grocery and butcher bill. (*He hands her a whole sheaf of bills speared on a nail.*) Now Mr. Schultz no give nasty looks with lamb chops.

(AUNTIE MAME *sinks to the ottoman in unbelieving gratitude. She stares at the spiked bills, which look like a ragged miniature Christmas tree.*)

AUNTIE MAME (*moved deeply*): You're both so dear to me. I'll pay you back someday—if I ever can. You know I will.

(NORAH *comes toward her, gently.*)

NORAH: You're a lovin' woman, mum. You're odd, but you're *lovin'!* And all we wish is you could find a *man.* As wonderful and lovin' and fine a gentleman as you are a fine lady. (*Thinking.*) Whatever happened to that nice Mr. Lindsay Woolsey? He was a dear soul.

AUNTIE MAME: He *was* a dear man, Norah. But I sent him away. I said no so many times when I had money, I couldn't say yes when I went broke.

(*At this moment,* YOUNG PAT *comes down the stairs, bursting with pride in his first long pants. He beams.*)

YOUNG PAT: Look!

(AUNTIE MAME *rises and crosses to the landing where he stands—almost as tall as she is.*)

AUNTIE MAME: Besides, I have my own fine gentleman, Norah. (*She holds up her wrist.*) Who buys me diamonds. (*Smiling.*) Or "almost" diamonds. (*In apparent high spirits,* AUNTIE MAME *moves blithely to the radio and snaps it on.*) What we need now is some music—some Christmas carols!

(*The radio squeals a little as she spins the dial through some spot announcements—finally coming to rest on a chorale version of "Deck the Halls with Boughs of Holly."*

AUNTIE MAME *starts to sing and directs the others to join in with her—which they do, enthusiastically joining hands and dancing in a circle.*)

ALL (*singing*):

"Deck the halls with boughs of holly,
Fa-la-la-la-la—la-la-la-la
'Tis the season to be jolly,
Fa-la-la-la-la—la-la-la-la."

(AUNTIE MAME *begins to break up. She turns away
from the others, trying to conceal her tears. This is
no season for her to be jolly.*

PAT, NORAH, *and* ITO *rally around trying to comfort
her.*)

YOUNG PAT (*hugging her*): Don't cry, Auntie Mame! Please
don't cry.

AUNTIE MAME (*trying to dry her tears*): Oh, hell, we don't
even have any Kleenex! (*But* NORAH *offers her apron
to* AUNTIE MAME, *and she uses it to wipe away the tears.
The doorbell chimes.* ITO *starts for the door.* AUNTIE
MAME *turns to* ITO.) If that's Santa Claus, tell him
we've already had it.

(ITO *ushers in the rubicund but apologetic figure of*
BEAUREGARD BURNSIDE. *He takes over in a generous
and expansive way, hardly giving anyone else an op-
portunity to speak.*)

BEAU: Ma'am, you don't know how happy I am to see you.

AUNTIE MAME (*uncertainly*): Well, I—

BEAU (*doffing his wide-brimmed hat*): Little lady, do you
know I've been skittlin' all over town trying to find
you? Do you realize there are ninety-seven Dennises in
the *Man*-hattan *Di*-rectory? And I was beginning to

worry you *might* live in that place over there called "Brooklyn."

AUNTIE MAME: But why did you—?

BEAU: I came to apologize. I told 'em right out it was all their fault, those Macy folk. A lady with your charm and refinement should have an executive position with a lot of hired help to rassle with all them pesky writin' and figurin' details. (*He starts toward the door.*) Will you excuse me a second, ma'am, while I skittle out and pay that cab driver so he can go home to his family?

AUNTIE MAME (*stunned*): You left a taxi meter running— in the middle of the Depression?

(BEAU *raises his hand in a benediction.*)

BEAU: Ma'am, when you're in oil, a stock market crash is somebody else's noise. (AUNTIE MAME *is nonplused.*) And if you wouldn't consider me *pre*-sumptious, I'd be most honored if you'd let me squire you out to dinner tonight.

AUNTIE MAME: No, thank you, we're just having a Christmas celebration, and I can't leave my little family.

BEAU: Ma'am, I like that. I like a woman who has feelin's about family. Why, I've got practically every kind of relative invented. You oughta come down Georgia-way and meet 'em all one day. You'd just love Peckerwood.

AUNTIE MAME: Peckerwood? Who's Peckerwood?

BEAU: Why, that's the name of my little ol' plantation. (*He turns and takes in* PAT, NORAH, *and* ITO *in an ex-*

pansive gesture.) Bring your little family along to dinner, ma'am; the more the merrier!

(AUNTIE MAME *is still spinning from the speed of all this*.)

AUNTIE MAME: But I'm not really dressed. . . .

BEAU (*at the door*): You look just fine to me, ma'am. A little powder on your nose, and you're just fine. I'll tell that taxi to wait.

(BEAU *exits. They all look at one another in excited bewilderment*.)

YOUNG PAT: He's nice—I like him!

AUNTIE MAME: Shh!

NORAH: Marry him, mum! The minute he asks you!

AUNTIE MAME: Norah, for God's sake!

YOUNG PAT: What's his name, Auntie Mame? You don't even know his name.

AUNTIE MAME (*wisely*): Yes, I do. Family, we are about to break bread with *Beauregard Jackson Pickett Burnside!* (NORAH *and* ITO *laugh delightedly. Swiftly* AUNTIE MAME *goes into action*.) Norah, get your coat. Ito, change your jacket. Where's my bag? (*She powders her nose as everyone flies around getting ready to go out*.) Patrick, wear your scarf—it's cold outside.

(NORAH *comes back in a scrubby cloth coat, carrying a corsage. She hands it to* AUNTIE MAME.)

NORAH: I was going to give you this wee thing at dinner.

AUNTIE MAME (*she pulls an ornament off the tree and pins it on* NORAH'S *coat*): Here's one for you, too.

(YOUNG PAT *appears in overcoat and muffler, and races for the door.*)

YOUNG PAT (*excitedly*): Come on! We hadn't ought to keep Mr. Burnside waiting!

(ITO *returns in a black alpaca coat.*)

ITO (*beaming*): Me never believe in Santa Claus. Me beginning to change mind.

AUNTIE MAME: Well, I never expected Santa Claus to have a Southern accent.

(*They all tear out the door,* AUNTIE MAME *bringing up the rear.*)

ANNOUNCER (*through the radio*): Merry Christmas from Manny, Moe, and Jack, your credit clothier!

AUNTIE MAME (*magnanimously, in a rich Southern accent*): Merry Christmas to you-all, Manny, Moe, and Jack! And a happy little ol' New Year!

(*She exits after the others, and the lights fade.*)

There is drippy Southern music. We bleed through the scrim to the picturesque tableau of the white-columned portico of the Burnside Mansion at Pecker-wood, with the aristocracy of Oglethorpe County posed gracefully on the lawn awaiting the arrival of AUNTIE MAME. *The scrim parts, and the stage comes alive with a twittering crowd of Southern belles and Georgia gentlemen, all dressed in Sunday best. A few wide white steps lead up to a veranda and a twin-leafed practical door. The front area is the lawn of Peckerwood, filled with bluegrass and bluebloods.*

This is a gathering of the clan to give the o.o. to UNCLE BEAU'S *Yankee girl friend. The tone is roughly the same as that with which General Sherman was received in Atlanta seventy years before.*

Prominent in the crowd is COUSIN JEFFERSON DAVIS CLAY PICKETT, *who booms like the cannons at Fort Sumter.*

COUSIN FAN, *a fussy, insecure poor relative, emerges from the house and twitters ineffectually around the veranda.*

COUSIN JEFF: Must be somethin' mighty special about this Dennis woman if'n Beau skittles her all the way down here from New York City. (*Turns to the veranda.*) Mornin', Cousin Fan.

COUSIN FAN: Peculiar mornin', Cousin Jeff. *Mighty* peculiar. Is it generally known that Beau and his lady friend have a *child* with 'em?

(*There are gasps, and a general reaction of shocked astonishment.*)

COUSIN JEFF: No-o-o-o!

COUSIN FAN: Don't think it's what you're thinkin'. The boy's thirteen, and Beau's only known her since Christmas. (*There is an air of disappointment at this.* COUSIN FAN *sniffs.*) Besides—she hain't even *met* Mother Burnside yet.

(*There is an eager reaction among the clan.*)

COUSIN JEFF: Ho-ho. Seems as if we're all right on time to see the fireworks.

COUSIN FAN: Well, you all know what a delicate *di*-gestive system Mother Burnside has. (*She rolls her eyes upward.* JEFF *turns confidentially to his wife.*)

COUSIN JEFF: Ho-ho. When she gets riled, ain't nobody in the State of Georgia—maybe in the whole Confederacy—can out-burp Mother Burnside.

(*The genteel chitchat freezes suddenly as* SALLY CATO

MACDOUGAL *floats in. This is a peaches-and-cream Southern belle. Every eye is on her. She is followed by her grubby little brother,* EMORY, *who is about* YOUNG PAT'S *age.*)

SALLY CATO: Well, now—!

COUSIN JEFF: Why, Sally Cato MacDougal!

SALLY CATO: Hello, Jeff honey.

COUSIN FAN: Didn't rightly 'spect *you* to be comin' round for the doin's.

SALLY (*dripping sweetness*): Why, however could I manage to stay away—when our own dear Beau is bringin' his little Yankee friend back down here to Peckerwood? Why, I wouldn't feel like a true daughter of the South if I didn't ooze out all the hospitality that's just simmerin' in my inners!

COUSIN JEFF: You're a bighearted woman, Sally Cato.

SALLY (*fluttery*): Well, now, jus' because Beauregard and me been engaged since grammar school don't mean I refrain from wishin' him and his new-found friend every happiness.

(YOUNG PAT *comes running on. He is slightly Lord Fauntleroyed. He stops short when he sees the crowd of people.*)

YOUNG PAT: My Auntie Mame—Miss Dennis, I mean—she says she'll be here in just a minute.

(SALLY CATO *smiles lovingly at* YOUNG PAT.)

SALLY: Well now—what a lovable, genteel little gentleman. (*She calls to her brother gutterally.*) Emory, come on over here. (*Back to* YOUNG PAT.) You and my little brother are gonna get along like a pair of colts in a pasture. I can just tell. (*She hits* EMORY *with her umbrella, then flutters among the guests.* EMORY *sullenly faces* YOUNG PAT.)

EMORY: What's your name, Yankee boy?

YOUNG PAT: Patrick Dennis.

EMORY: If ya gimme a dime, I'll take you down to my shanty and show ya my dirty pitchas.

YOUNG PAT: Maybe I'd better not—right now. (*Making conversation.*) Your sister's nice.

EMORY (*incredulous*): *Nice?!* You're plumb crazy. They teach ya to spell up there, Yankee boy?

YOUNG PAT: Sure.

EMORY (*lowering his voice*): My sister is a B-I-T-C-H.

(*There is a clatter and rumble from within the portals of Peckerwood.* MOTHER BURNSIDE'S *gravelly baritone is raised in acid invective.*)

MOTHER BURNSIDE'S VOICE (*off*): Where's my soda tablets? What son of a no-good-hound-dog stole my soda tablets?

BEAU'S VOICE (*also from off*): They're right in your lap, Mother.

(*All turn toward the double doors, which* COUSIN FAN *opens timidly.* BEAU *pushes a wheel chair on to the veranda; in the wheel chair sits* MOTHER BURNSIDE, *a beady-eyed, imperious woman built along the lines of a General Electric refrigerator. Dressed all in black,*

she looks like a cross between Caligula and a cockatoo.
Everybody proffers a tentative greeting.)

MOTHER BURNSIDE: Beauregard, when you gonna trot out that New York filly? (*Her beady eyes scan the assemblage contemptuously.*) All I can see around here is *family.*

ALL: Mornin', Mother Burnside.

MOTHER BURNSIDE (*suddenly brightens*): 'Ceptin' you, Sally Cato. Still paintin' your fingernails?

SALLY: You're lookin' cute as a bug, Miz Burnside. (MOTHER BURNSIDE *burps.*) Well, welcome home, Beau darlin'!

BEAU (*uncomfortably*): Hello there, Sally Cato.

MOTHER BURNSIDE (*to* BEAU, *wagging her head*): When we got peaches right there, ripe for the pickin', I cain't see why any man would go hankerin' after some *Northern* alligator pear. (*She clasps a hand to her stomach, as if a gastritic eruption were about to take place.*)

BEAU (*worried*): Now, now, Mama—let's keep our hominy grits goin' the right way! (*He calls off.*) Mame? Mame honey, we're all out here, waitin' for you.

AUNTIE MAME'S VOICE (*from off. Calls, Southern as a candied yam*): Ah'm comin', Beau-sugah. Ah'm just bustin' to meet yoah sweet little ol' mothah! (MAME *swirls on, wearing a hoop skirt and looking very much like Scarlett O'Hara. She stops, with a little gasp.*)

BEAU: Mother, may I present Miss Mame Dennis?

(AUNTIE MAME *falters only for a fraction of a second,*

then advances up the steps of the veranda and takes
MOTHER BURNSIDE's *leathery hand.*)

AUNTIE MAME: I don't mind sayin', Miz Burnside, you're
everything I ever expected and quite a bit more.

(MOTHER BURNSIDE *burps.*)

BEAU (*waving across the lawn*): And these are all my kin-
folk. That's my cousin, Jefferson Davis Clay Pickett;
his wife; Cousin Fan; Aunt Euphemia; Uncle Moultrie; Lizzie Beaufort—you'll get to know 'em all.
You'll all be first-namin' each other soon as we pour
another gallon o' bourbon into the punch bowl! (BEAU
exits into the house.)

AUNTIE MAME: I cain't tell you how chowmin' it is to meet
all of you-all! (*This doesn't sound quite right to her,
but she carries it off nicely.*)

(SALLY *swoops up, taking* MAME's *hands with a gush
of affection.*)

SALLY: And I'm Sally Cato MacDougal. I could just tell
from the first *instant* I set eyes on you that we was
gonna be the *closest* of bosom friends, Mame. May
I call you Mame?

AUNTIE MAME: Please do.

SALLY: You call me "Sally Cato," heah?—All my most intimate friends *do.*

(*Several glances are exchanged.* AUNTIE MAME *is completely taken in.*)

AUNTIE MAME: Why, that's awfully kind of you, Sally Cato.

SALLY: Was it *horses* brought you and Beauregard together?

AUNTIE MAME (*blankly*): Horses?

SALLY: Well, I can't imagine Beau even *lookin'* at a lady who wasn't practically *bawn* on a horse.

AUNTIE MAME (*laying it on*): Oh, I just love riding. Up in New York hardly a day goes by that I don't have the sadd—the *boots* on. Up every morning at the crack of dawn for a brisk canter through Central Park.

SALLY: Well, now—that settles it. Here I've been wrackin' my poor brain tryin' to figure what *special* I could do to let you know how I feel about your bein' down here. And what could be better than a *hunt!*

AUNTIE MAME (*paling a little*): A hunt???

SALLY (*raising her voice*): Listen, evabodeh! Beauregard's gone and *surprised* us all! It seems Miz Dennis here is a prominent North'n horsewoman.

AUNTIE MAME (*trying to put the brakes on this*): Well, I wouldn't say *prominent*—No, I'm not prominent.

SALLY (*barreling on*): So natcherly we'll have to have a hunt! Dawn, tomorrow morning! And evabody's invited! (*She turns brightly to* AUNTIE MAME.) Won't we have the lark, all of us—at sunup—leapin' over those hedges, jumpin' over those river gaps, the hounds yappin' around those boulders—(AUNTIE MAME *steadies herself against one of the columns.*) I tell you, Mame, every eye in this county is going to be on you tomorrow mornin'!

AUNTIE MAME (*thinking fast*): If I'd only *known*. You see, I didn't bring down any of my ridin' togs.

SALLY: Don't you worry, Mame child. I've got *dozens* of things you could wear. What's your shoe size?

(MAME *tries to draw her feet under her skirt.*)

AUNTIE MAME (*lying*): Three-B.

SALLY: Marvelous. Same as I wear. I can even fit you out with boots.

AUNTIE MAME (*weakly*): I don't know if Beau would want me to—

SALLY (*barreling on*): You *do* ride astride, Mame dear?

AUNTIE MAME (*a hopeful gleam in her eyes*): No, no. Side-saddle—always. Daddy, the Colonel, insisted that I learn it. He said it was the only way for a true lady to ride. So graceful. Silly of him, of course, because *nobody* rides sidesaddle these days, but it's the only way I know how. (*She sighs, pleased with herself.*)

SALLY (*purring*): Now, isn't that grand! I just happen to have a little old sidesaddle that'll do you *fine*.

(BEAU *comes out on the lawn again, carrying a trayful of punch glasses. Graciously he passes them around to the guests.*)

BEAU: Refreshment, ladies?

(MAME *drinks a whole punch cup at one gulp.*)

SALLY: Beau darlin', we're havin' ourselves a hunt! At dawn tomorrow! And you want to hear somethin' fantastic? Your sweet little Yankee girl is gonna ride sidesaddle.

BEAU: I won't allow it! It's too dangerous.

SALLY: But, darlin', she's insisted.

BEAU: Well, anything Mame says she can do, she can do. I
tell you—this is an amazing woman.

(MAME *quickly downs a second drink.*)

SALLY CATO: Oh, Mame sugah—I'm just goin' to *hold my
breath* until dawn tomorrow.

AUNTIE MAME: Do that, honey.

(*The lights fade.*)

The lighting makes a transition to dawn. In the distance a grumpy rooster crows. The lights come up on one of the side areas, which is the bedroom of the bridal cottage. AUNTIE MAME *is behind a screen, struggling into riding gear.* YOUNG PAT *has a book in his hand.*

AUNTIE MAME: Stop looking at the pictures and read it to me, darling; I'm listening.

(YOUNG PAT *sits backward on a chair and turns to the opening page.*)

YOUNG PAT: "How to Ride a Horse." (*She is struggling to get into a pair of borrowed riding boots.* YOUNG PAT *begins to read.*) It says you should always get on a horse from the left side.

AUNTIE MAME: *Your* left side or the *horse's* left side?

YOUNG PAT: It doesn't say. Listen to this. (*He reads.*) "Whenever a rider approaches a strange mount"—I guess that means the horse—"he should fix the animal

in the eye with a masterful gaze. For a horse can de-
tect the slightest indication of trepidation." (*He
breaks off.*) What's "trepidation"?

AUNTIE MAME: That's what your Auntie Mame's got a bad
case of right now. Go on, dear, go on.

YOUNG PAT: "The horse is extremely sensitive—"

AUNTIE MAME: Where??????????

YOUNG PAT: There are some peachy pictures in this book
about how to jump over fences. It says you should
lean.

AUNTIE MAME: If anybody does any leaning, it's gotta be
the horse. (*She tries vainly to pull on one of the boots.
After a painful groan, she stops, closes her eyes, and
mutters something inarticulately under her breath.*)

YOUNG PAT: What did you say, Auntie Mame?

AUNTIE MAME: I'm not talking to you, my little love. I'm
talking to God. (*She emerges in riding skirt and tight
boots. She can hardly walk.*) I think Sally Cato left a
foot in this one.

YOUNG PAT: I'll help you. (AUNTIE MAME *sits on the be-
flowered bed and* PAT *tries to shove the boot on.*)

AUNTIE MAME: So this is what they call "dying with your
boots on."

YOUNG PAT (*sympathetically*): Why are you going through
all this, Auntie Mame?

AUNTIE MAME (*distantly*): Darling, if I can only snag you
an Uncle Beau, all our problems will be solved. (*She
makes a wistful half smile.*) Besides, there's one other
extremely minor, relatively unimportant little old
thing: I happen to be in love with him.

(YOUNG PAT *laughs happily.*)

YOUNG PAT: Has he asked you anything yet?

AUNTIE MAME (*shaking her head*): No. But he wouldn't have brought us down here—if he didn't intend to.

(*There is a knock at the door.*)

BEAU (*from off*): Are you dressed yet, Mame, honey?

(YOUNG PAT *quickly hides the book behind him.*)

AUNTIE MAME: Oh, come in, Beau darlin'. (*He enters, resplendent in a red riding habit. He has several cameras draped about his neck.*) Oh my, how handsome you look.

BEAU: Likewise, Mame. Hold it! (MAME *strikes a fancy pose. He snaps a picture.*) You are now im-mortalized in cell-you-loid. (*He turns to* YOUNG PAT.) Would you excuse us for a second, young fella? There's something I want to talk to your Auntie Mame about.

YOUNG PAT (*obligingly*): Oh, sure. (*He scoots out of the room.*)

BEAU (*taking a deep breath*): Mame, what I've got to say, I've got to say fast, a-fore that huntin' horn blows. And talkin' fast is somethin' that don't come easy to a South'n gentleman.

AUNTIE MAME: Then talk slow, Beau darlin'—I can listen fast.

(BEAU *takes her hand.*)

BEAU: I consider myself a very lucky man. It was luck that made me smell oil when I was walkin' across that soybean patch Cousin Marvin left me. And it was just pure dumb Georgia luck that roller-skated us together last Christmas.

AUNTIE MAME (*hanging on every word*): I feel the same way, Beau dear. Go on.

(*He kneels.*)

BEAU: Mame, honey—what I want to ask you is—(*He is beginning to get red-faced.*) Would you—Could you —That is, *might* you—(*She turns away coyly. The hunting horn sounds blatantly, off.* BEAU *reacts like a fireman who has heard the bell. He drops* MAME'S *hand abruptly.*) To the hounds!

(*He bolts off eagerly.* MAME *is left alone in the bedroom.*)

AUNTIE MAME: Hounds! Sons-of-bitches.

(*Her shoulders sag as the lights fade. The bedroom is scrimmed out in the momentary darkness, and then the lights come up on the portico, columns, and front lawn of Peckerwood.*)

The red-coated huntsman comes on and blows an-other blast on the hunting horn.

BEAU *and* COUSIN JEFF *come on, ready for the hunt.*

BEAU (*taking a deep breath of morning air*): Can't wait to get on the trail of that fox. We *got* a fox, ain't we, Jeff?

JEFF: Had to use that spare one we was keepin' in the cellar of the icehouse. He's a mite moth-eaten, but he'll do.

(SALLY CATO *comes on, assured in her riding habit. She crosses right to* BEAU *and fiddles with his ascot.*)

SALLY: Beau darlin'—now, ain't you just the *handsomest* little old thing.

BEAU (*embarrassed*): Aw-w-w, Sally Cato. (*Turns, searching*). Hope we got Mame a nice piece of horseflesh.

SALLY (*patting* BEAU'S *lapel cozily*): Don't you worry one minute 'bout your sweet little ol' Northern gal. I puhsonally picked her mount. I've seen to it that she's gonna be took care of just fine. (*She smiles at him with every tooth in her head.*)

BEAU: You're a bighearted woman, Sally Cato. (*There is a gentle whinny from off.* BEAU *crosses, calling to the grooms.*) Hold her steady, boy! (*Reaches in his pocket.*) I got a lump of sugar for you, Brown Beauty, old girl! (*He goes off, and we hear him mounting—the creak of leather and pawing in the gravel.*)

BEAU'S VOICE (*to the horse, amiably*): Hup—hup. Atta girl!

(SALLY CATO *slaps her whip on the ground and laughs.*

AUNTIE MAME *comes out of the house, followed by* YOUNG PAT. *She's putting up a brave front, and he is still reading from the book, instructing her. She actually manages to smile at* SALLY CATO *as she tries to fake the walk and stance of an experienced horse-woman.*)

AUNTIE MAME: Mornin', Sally Cato.

SALLY (*sweetly*): Mornin', Mame dear. How unusual you look. (*Calls off.*) You can bring up Miss Dennis' horse now, boys. (*Back to* MAME.) He's the most special thing in mah stable; evahbody talks about him. What an exhilaratin' day we're gonna have. (*She starts off toward the mounting block offstage.*)

AUNTIE MAME: Just a minute, Sally Cato—wouldn't my horse like it if I called him by his name? What's his name?

SALLY (*smiling*): Lightnin' Rod.

(SALLY CATO *goes off.* AUNTIE MAME *looks struck.*)

GIRL: Mawnin', Miss Dennis. (*She skips.*)

AUNTIE MAME: Mawnin'! Mawnin'! (*She imitates the girl's skip.*)

YOUNG PAT (*concerned*): Auntie Mame—could you maybe . . . sprain your ankle—quick?

AUNTIE MAME (*grimly*): I've got to go through with it. I can't be a disgrace to Beau in front of all his people.

(*There is a fierce whinnying off, and wild stomping.*

TWO GROOMS *back onto the stage in panic; one has his upstage hand hidden in his coat.*

There is a babble of VOICES, *onstage and off.*)

VOICES: Ho! Rein him up. Stand clear of that horse, boy. Steady, steady!

(AUNTIE MAME *stares off, horrified.*)

AUNTIE MAME (*dry-throated*): That—that—that horse's name isn't . . . Lightnin' Rod?

GROOM (*nods portentously*): Lightnin' Rod.

(*Again the offstage horse thunders a whinny and paws the gravel.*)

AUNTIE MAME (*swallows*): Maybe if I gave him a lump of sugar, it would—

(*The* GROOM *lifts up his bandaged hand.*)

GROOM: I wouldn't try it if I was you, ma'am.

(MAME *kisses* PAT *good-by, then edges toward the off-stage animal, trying to stare it down.*)

AUNTIE MAME (*muttering to herself*): "Fix the animal in

the eye with a masterful gaze—" (*She goes off like Sidney Carton en route to the guillotine. There is more pawing and whinnying, accompanied by shouts and grunts, as she presumably manages to get aboard the horse.*)

(YOUNG PAT *watches with horrified fascination.*

COUSIN FAN *helps on the bloodthirsty figure of* MOTHER BURNSIDE, *who has a pair of field glasses. She sits in the rocker.*)

MOTHER BURNSIDE (*looking down toward where the horse is stomping*): Naow, that is what I call a spirited ani-mule! (AUNTIE MAME, *off, lets out a fading scream, as the horse hoofs gallop away.* MOTHER BURNSIDE *waves a dirty old lace handkerchief delightedly.*) Good-by, Yankee Girl!

(*The* HUNTSMAN'S *horn sounds off, and the hunt is evidently in progress.*

MOTHER BURNSIDE *glues the field glasses to her eyes. She rocks delightedly through the following.*

EMORY *dashes on.* YOUNG PAT *has leaped up onto the veranda and watches tiptoe, clutching one of the col-umns.* EMORY *rushes up to him and grabs his arm.*)

EMORY: Hey, Yankee Boy! I seen 'em sidesaddlin' up Lightnin' Rod. Your aunt ain't plannin' to ride him, is she?

YOUNG PAT: Plannin'? Look!

(EMORY *climbs the other column.*)

EMORY: Kee-ripes. Look at 'em go.

YOUNG PAT: Auntie Mame! Fall off! Fall off!

(*The sound of progressing hunt comes from three staggered speakers on the balcony rail. We hear stereophonically the yapping of the dogs and the pounding of horses' hoofs and the occasional bleat of the* HUNTSMAN'S *horn.*

MOTHER BURNSIDE'S *field glasses follow the action and she rocks vigorously and chortles with grisly good humor, punctuated by burps.*)

MOTHER BURNSIDE: Cleared the first hedgerow and not a broken leg yit! Look at 'em go! What's she comin' back this way for? That fool Yankee girl's got 'em goin' in circles. (YOUNG PAT, EMORY, COUSIN FAN, MOTHER BURNSIDE, *and two of the* GROOMS *are watching in fascinated horror.*) Get out of my flower garden. Keep them damn horses out of my Bougainvillia. Look out fer that yar flood wall!

YOUNG PAT: Lean, Auntie Mame—lean!

(COUSIN FAN *and* YOUNG PAT *cover their eyes—then peek out, fearing the worst.*)

MOTHER BURNSIDE: Gol dang if that Yankee gal didn't sail right over it! *No hands!*

GROOM: She's passin' everybody!

MOTHER BURNSIDE: She's passin' the Mastuh of the Hounds! (*She puts down the glasses angrily.*) Mighty bad form, passin' the Mastuh!

(*The glasses go up again and sweep along, following the action.*)

YOUNG PAT: She's passin' the dogs!

MOTHER BURNSIDE (*astounded*): Mother of Jefferson Davis, she's passin' the *fox!*

(MOTHER BURNSIDE *rocks as if she herself were in the saddle. Off, we hear the wheezing of a Model-A Ford approaching at top speed, honking, and screeching of brakes. There is a car-door slam off, and the* VET *rushes on. He has a gun in a holster, and his face is livid with rage.*)

VET (*roaring accusation*): Miz Burnside! Is that hawse out thar Lightnin' Rod???

MOTHER BURNSIDE (*delighted*): Suah looks like it. (*To the* VET.) But we won't need a hawse doctah around here today. We're gonna need the othah kind!

VET (*thundering*): Plain premeditated *murdah,* that's what it is!

(*He points toward the progressing fox hunt, which has apparently zigzagged several times across the field of vision from the portico. Suddenly* MOTHER BURNSIDE *stops rocking and leans forward. Now all the watchers freeze, staring dead-front in horror.*

The sound of hoofs, hounds, and cries grow louder, as if the hunting party were advancing straight upon them.)

MOTHER BURNSIDE (*shrieks*): That damn Yankee Girl is leadin' 'em straight into the livin' room!

(But it is a near miss. All eyes swing toward offstage the opposite side from which the hunt departed, but the same side on which the VET'S *car is parked. The noise of the approaching hunt grows louder still.*

YOUNG PAT *covers his eyes.* COUSIN FAN *shrieks.* MOTHER BURNSIDE *braces one leg against the railing.)*

VET *(screaming, his arm raised)*: Watch out—my flivvah's parked in back of them begonia bushes! That's caounty property! That's—

GROOM: Rein her in!

(There's a mighty crash of hoofs against glass and tin; there is the outraged "Ah-oo-gah" of an old Ford horn, which subsides into a dying gasp.)

YOUNG PAT *(cries out)*: Auntie Mame!!!!!

(Almost as if hurtled onto the stage, AUNTIE MAME *staggers forward.*

She is windblown and disheveled. In one hand she has the broken steering wheel from the VET'S *car. She is holding something in her other hand, but it is hidden behind the folds of her skirt.)*

MOTHER BURNSIDE: What happened to the fox?

AUNTIE MAME *(holding aloft the limp fur piece that was once a fox)*: Trampled him to death!

(The others from the hunt begin to pour on, babbling with astonishment, congratulating the dazed AUNTIE MAME. BEAU *rushes up to her.)*

BEAU: Are you all right, Mame honey? When I saw that

crazy hawse crash into that car, and you flyin' through the air—

(AUNTIE MAME *lamely holds up the steering wheel.*)

AUNTIE MAME: If I hadn't grabbed hold of this, I'd be in North Carolina!

(SALLY CATO *comes on uncertainly. But everybody is gathered around* AUNTIE MAME *admiringly.*)

JEFF: Soo-*pub* hawse-woman! Pufeckly soo-*pub!*

VET (*turning on* SALLY CATO): Sally Cato MacDougal, as County veterinarian, Ah *commanded* you two years ago to have that crazy Lightnin' Rod destroyed. Why, she oughta have her name read outta every huntin' pack in the who' county.

BEAU (*turning his back on* SALLY CATO *and swelling with pride close to* AUNTIE MAME): Everybody—ah want you to meet my little *Yankee Valkyrie!*

(*They embrace. The* VET *shakes his fist at* SALLY CATO.

AUNTIE MAME *is mounting the steps of the veranda, blushing prettily at the flood of compliments.*)

JEFF: What a seat that woman has! What a magnificent seat!

(AUNTIE MAME *glances back with a startled take. Then she touches the back of her skirt to see if it's torn there.*)

BEAU (*bounding up the stairs, stretching out his arms*): Listen, evahbodeh! I have an impohtant announcement to make to you-all! This magnificent Diana-of-the-Chase is gonna become Mrs. Beauregard Jackson Pickett Burnside!

(AUNTIE MAME *tosses the fox to* SALLY *like a bridal bouquet.*)

SALLY: Emory, come on home!

EMORY (*happily*): Hot damn! Mah sistah's gonna bust a gut! (*He skeedaddles off, following his sister.*)

MOTHER BURNSIDE: Well, what are you-all standin' around for??? Skittle yo' selves into the house and we'll all have a *glass o' whisky!* Come on.

(COUSIN FAN *helps* MOTHER BURNSIDE *back through the French doors. All congratulate the beaming* BEAU *and the beat-up but victorious* AUNTIE MAME *as they file into the house.*

Nobody's paying much attention to YOUNG PAT, *and he hangs back unnoticed. All the guests have gone inside now. On the steps,* BEAU *takes* AUNTIE MAME'S *hand.*)

BEAU: Ah'll make you happy, Mame honey. For a honeymoon, we'll take a year off and go clean around the world! Just you and me. (*He embraces her.*)

(YOUNG PAT, *hearing this, slips farther downstage, feeling very much alone.*

AUNTIE MAME *starts to go in the house with* BEAU *but suddenly she glances back and sees* YOUNG PAT.)

AUNTIE MAME (*to* BEAU): You go in the house, darlin'. I'll be there in just a minute. (BEAU *exits.* AUNTIE

MAME *crosses quickly to* YOUNG PAT, *sympathetically*.)
Patrick, my little love—

YOUNG PAT (*softly*): Congratulations, Auntie Mame.

(*She takes* YOUNG PAT's *hand and leads him to the steps. She sits, holding him, though he hangs back a bit*.)

AUNTIE MAME: Your Auntie Mame's in love—and very, very happy.

YOUNG PAT: I won't see you for a long time.

AUNTIE MAME: But, darling, you'll be busy at school. And I'll write you every day. I promise. And I'll be back with you before you even know it. Now, come on in the house and we'll have some breakfast. And let me see you smile. I haven't gone yet. Up! Up! That's my boy.

(PAT *manages a small smile*.)

YOUNG PAT: Can I ask you just one question? (*She nods*.) How did you stay on that horse?

AUNTIE MAME: It was just like the bracelet in New Haven: I got stuck. (*She reaches behind her, confidentially*.) But at the other end!

(*They laugh warmly, and* AUNTIE MAME *gives* PATRICK *a big hug and they go into the house together*.)

The curtain falls.

Act Two

*In the darkness we hear an uncertain blend of ex-boy
sopranos singing the "St. Boniface Fight Song."*

BOYS' VOICES (*unseen, singing*):
   "Fight, fight, fight for St. Boniface, Boniface!
   We will win for St. Boniface, Boniface!
   Carry the ball over the line!
   Show 'em what we can do!
   Fight, fight, fight for St. Boniface Blue!"

*As the music fades, the right half of the traveler is
drawn off and the lights come up on:*

A study room at St. Boniface Academy, an inset right.

YOUNG PAT *is seated at a study table wearing a beanie.
He looks taller and older, but this is the same lad who
gave* AUNTIE MAME'S *life a purpose and direction in
Act One. But somehow the ingenuous charm of child-
hood seems to have worn off a bit. There is a trace of
cockiness and conceit about* YOUNG PAT *now, and*

occasionally he shows a faint resemblance to a MR.
BABCOCK *who has been shrunk in the laundry.*

YOUNG PAT *is checking over a letter he has written.*

YOUNG PAT (*reading*): "To Mrs. Mame Burnside, American Express, Cairo. Dear Auntie Mame. It's wonderful
to get your letters every day. Thank you for the chop-
sticks you sent from Yokohama. They sure come in
handy. I guess you and Uncle Beau are enjoying the
world all right—and vice versa." (*He makes an in-
sertion in longhand.*) Ha, ha—joke. (*He continues
reading.*) "Mr. Babcock says if I work hard here at
Saint Boniface he will enroll me at Rumson University, which is Mr. Babcock's alma mater. He says I'll be
very lucky if I'm admitted—considering everything."
(*He turns over the page to read the other side.*) "I
plan to spend the holidays again with the Babcocks in
Darien. Junior Babcock and I have swell times there,
and I have met the kids from practically all the best
families in Connecticut. Your loving nephew, Patrick."

(*As the lights fade, we hear a haunting muezzin cry,
and the right half of the traveler closes in front of*
YOUNG PAT'S *study room.*)

The action is continuous, as the traveler opens in front of the area stage left, revealing:

The Pyramids. This is an inset, with levels, suggesting the slope of the great Pyramid, with others vaguely along the horizon.

We find UNCLE BEAU *in a pith helmet and wearing a garland of Leicas and light meters. He has climbed above* AUNTIE MAME *to shoot down at her as she studies* YOUNG PAT'S *letter. She is garbed in a fetching camel driver's outfit from Russek's, and scowls slightly as she reads aloud.*

AUNTIE MAME (*reading*): "Junior Babcock and I have swell times there, and I have met the kids from practically all the best families in Connecticut." (*She calls up to* BEAU.) Oh, dear, Beau—I have a feeling we should be getting back.

UNCLE BEAU (*fiddling with his camera*): Just one more shot.

AUNTIE MAME: Home, I mean. I feel Patrick needs me.

UNCLE BEAU: Move a little to the right, Mame darlin'. I'm gettin' too much pyramid and not enough you.

AUNTIE MAME: Beau. I do wish you'd stop climbing up on things. It makes me so nervous.

UNCLE BEAU: Remember, the higher you go, the more interesting the shot. Now, look natural. (AUNTIE MAME *strikes a* Vogue *cover pose and puts on a frozen smile.*) Oh, that's just fine. (*He clicks the picture, fussing inexpertly with the camera.*) You know, Mame, I think that's gonna turn out even better than the one of you standing by the ol' Moulmein Pagoda, looking eastward to the sea.

AUNTIE MAME: Now, you come down from there. (*As he does, she takes his arm affectionately.*) Little did I think when I married you that I was getting such a wonderful photographer, too. (*Lightly.*) Oh, did you remember to put film in the camera this time?

UNCLE BEAU: I sure did! (*He opens the camera to make sure, and the entire roll of exposed film unreels itself in the bright Egyptian sunlight.*) Dang!

(*The lights fade, and the traveler closes across the Pyramid area, left. In the momentary darkness we hear the strains of the Rumson University alma mater.*)

GLEE CLUB (*singing from off*):
    "O, Rumson U, dear Rumson U,
    To you we'll e'er be staunch and true.
    And when our college days are o'er,
    We'll remember thee forever more."

The traveler opens on the area right, and the lights come up on:

A dormitory room at Rumson University. This is an inset, right. The action is continuous.

Several years have passed, and for the first time we see PATRICK DENNIS, *the young man. He lounges casually at a typewriter, with textbooks littering the desk in front of him. However, he is engaged in the happy pastime of writing another letter to his* AUNTIE MAME. *He wears a beanie blazoned with the Rumson "R." He has matured into a remarkably handsome, intelligent, and personable young man. There's only one trouble: he knows it. Pulling the letter from the typewriter,* PATRICK *reads.*

PATRICK (*reading*): "To Mrs. Beauregard Jackson Pickett Burnside, care of American Express, Zurich, Switzerland. Dear Auntie Mame. I think it's great that you and Uncle Beau are getting an eighth honeymoon on your eighth anniversary. Everybody here was certainly impressed with the statue of the laughing Buddha you sent me from Siam. It was a bit large, however, to get through the door of the dorm.

"If you decide to go on that caravan to Baghdad, don't let them give you a camel named 'Lightnin' Rod.'

"Rumson U. is not as dull and denominational as you thought. Miss Pritchard's finishing school is nearby, and it's overflowing with the prettiest debutantes you ever saw. Since you came and spent my last vacation with me, I have grown several more inches, my voice has changed several more times—and you may not recognize what my glands have done to me. (*He turns the page over.*) Give Uncle Beau a kiss for me; I'm sure he will enjoy it more coming from you since I've been shaving almost daily now and my beard tickles. (*A thought occurs to him and he pencils an insert into the letter.*) . . . or so the debs tell me. (*He chuckles at his own joke, then continues reading.*) Say 'Hi' to the Matterhorn for me. Your loving nephew, Patrick."

(*The lights fade, and the traveler closes right. From off we hear some hyperbolic yodeling.*)

The Matterhorn. The levels which represented the Pyramids have been redressed and masked to depict an Alpine glacier.

UNCLE BEAU *is actually out of sight amid the peaks high above* AUNTIE MAME, *who is decked out in stunning fur parka, and reads* PATRICK'S *letter. Again, the action is nearly continuous.*

AUNTIE MAME (*reading*): Glands . . . Debutantes! (*She calls up to* UNCLE BEAU, *who is out of sight above.*) Beau, I have a feeling that Patrick's right on the brink of something.

UNCLE BEAU (*still out of sight*): Just a little higher, and I think this is gonna be the best shot yet! Mame, honey, do you mind stepping back a bit?

(AUNTIE MAME *looks over her shoulder and down behind her. From the expression on her face, we know it is a sheer drop of half a mile straight down. She calls up to* BEAU, *sweetly.*)

AUNTIE MAME: I'd rather not.

UNCLE BEAU: Don't you never mind—I'll skittle up a mite.

AUNTIE MAME: Please, Beau, no higher.

UNCLE BEAU: Remember, honey, the high shots are the best. (AUNTIE MAME *starts to protest, but we see an ice axe being lowered from above.*) Take this, honey. Pesky thing keeps gettin' in my way.

AUNTIE MAME (*taking it, gingerly*): No! Hang on to the other end, dear, for your balance.

UNCLE BEAU (*off stage. Calling down*): Don't you worry, Mame—I'm as sure-footed as a mountain goat. Hold it—just like that! Steady—wait'll I refocus.

(*Again* MAME *strikes a pose, while* BEAU *yodels blithely. But suddenly the yodel resolves into a thin, fading scream that reverberates down the glacier.*)

AUNTIE MAME (*tentatively*): Beau? (*The other end of the rope drops with limp significance.* AUNTIE MAME *looks up, horrified.*) BEAU!!!!!

(*The lights fade quickly and the travelers close.*

Melancholy voices from backstage hum "Massa's in the Cold, Cold Ground," with a wistful yodel in counterpoint.

Pinwheel projections spin on the closed travelers, suggesting a lapse of time.)

The Beekman Place apartment.

There are dust covers over some of the chairs. LIND-SAY, *who is graying nicely into a sort of Manhattan Ronald Colman, adjusts a Dictaphone.* VERA, *who is now somewhere between forty and death, has not aged at all—due to the diurnal ministrations of Charles of the Ritz.*

VERA (*looking at* LINDSAY *skeptically*): What's that thing supposed to be, Lindsay?

LINDSAY: A Dictaphone.

VERA: She'll never use it. You've lugged all this junk in here for nothing.

LINDSAY: Vera, she can't go on living in a vacuum. Mame's always got to have a project!

VERA: She's got a project. Now she's the tragic queen, and she's having such fun being miserable. All she's done for two years is wander around Europe revisiting the places she's been with Beau. Eight times she climbed that lousy Matterhorn—to toss rose petals down the glacier.

LINDSAY: Well, she must have loved him.

(VERA *starts to take off some of the dust covers.*)

VERA: Let's get some more of these dust covers off—the place looks like the Main Chapel at Campbell's.

(LINDSAY *helps her.*)

LINDSAY: You know, Vera, I'm a coward—I should've gone to the boat to meet her.

(VERA *is prowling for a drink. The door buzzer rings.* LINDSAY *crosses to open the door for* AGNES GOOCH, *a dowdy, owl-eyed secretary who slouches in the foyer with a shorthand pad under her arm.*)

VERA: I haven't seen her since I dragged myself over for the funeral. Wasn't it just like Mame to keep him till I got there? (*Looking at the label of the lone bottle.*) Southern Comfort. Oh, well.

LINDSAY (*at the door, to* GOOCH): Oh, yes—come in.

VERA (*turning from the bar, expectantly*): Mame? (GOOCH *schlumps into the apartment.* VERA's *jaw drops.*) My God, she can't have changed *that* much!

GOOCH (*in a flat, nasal drone*): I'm from Speed-o.

VERA (*blankly*): What?

LINDSAY: I called this secretarial service. I want to show Mame we really mean business, let her know I'm really serious about this thing. (*Turning to* GOOCH.) Your name is . . . ?

GOOCH: Agnes Gooch.

LINDSAY: Now, Miss Gooch, you'll be taking dictation from Mrs. Burnside—and she's a pretty fast talker.

GOOCH: Oh, Speed-o won't let anybody out who can't do at least a hundred words a minute. (*She lowers her eyes modestly.*) I'm over two hundred.

VERA: You're not! Well, if Mame does any dictating— which I doubt—it'll be sprinkled with French, Egyptian, Japanese, and four-letter words.

GOOCH (*after a moment's thought*): I'm afraid I'm not your girl. (GOOCH *starts to leave, but* LINDSAY *moves to stop her.*)

LINDSAY: Please stay, Miss Gooch. This should be an interesting experience for you. Mrs. Burnside will pour out a flood of words and ideas, and you must soak them all up. You'll be her . . . (*He gropes for the word.*) Her *sponge!*

(GOOCH *looks at* LINDSAY *askance.* VERA *throws up her hands.*)

VERA: Oh, Lindsay, how can Mame write a book? She can't even sit still long enough to write a post card.

LINDSAY (*leading* GOOCH *toward the desk*): I've got somebody to help her. (*He glances at his watch.*) Oh, good Lord, I told the fellow to be here at three o'clock.

VERA (*interested*): What fellow?

LINDSAY: Miss Gooch, you're on salary as of right now.

(AUNTIE MAME *and* PATRICK *appear in the foyer. She is in black, and* PATRICK *wears his Ivy League best. They have been chatting warmly.* PATRICK *presses the buzzer three times.*)

AUNTIE MAME: Why are you ringing, Patrick? Don't you have a key?

PATRICK: Of course. I forgot.

(*Within the apartment, LINDSAY springs into excited action.*)

LINDSAY: Three buzzes—that's the signal! (*He herds VERA and GOOCH out the door leading to the terrace.*) Come on—we're going to surprise her.

VERA: Oh, you're acting like a schoolboy.

(*LINDSAY comes back for GOOCH, who has started toward the foyer door.*)

LINDSAY: You too! (*He pulls her off right.*)

(*PATRICK ushers MAME in, just as the others vanish. They are carrying parcels.*)

PATRICK: Welcome home, Auntie Mame.

(*AUNTIE MAME looks about the room with a dramatic remoteness.*)

AUNTIE MAME: Dear old Beekman Place. It's so loyal. No matter how far I go, it just sits here and waits for me. You know, I rather expected Vera at the boat.

PATRICK: I wouldn't let her come. I wanted to be alone with you. (*They hug.*)

AUNTIE MAME: Patrick, my little Patrick. Now open your presents. Oh, Patrick, every time I see you you get taller and more grown up.

(*PATRICK tears open a package and is baffled as he takes out a pair of Bavarian leather walking shorts.*

AUNTIE MAME *holds them up against him. With a grin* PATRICK *remembers a similar gift of many years before.*)

PATRICK: Golly, short pants—at last! Can I try 'em on right now, Auntie Mame? Right now?

(*They both laugh—but* AUNTIE MAME's *attitude changes instantly as* VERA *and* LINDSAY *burst into the room.*)

LINDSAY: Surprise! Surprise, Mame!

VERA: Surprise, darling—welcome home!

(AUNTIE MAME *is now Duse, playing the Tragic Muse for the benefit of* VERA.)

AUNTIE MAME (*kissing* VERA *lightly on the cheek*): Vera, dear. And staunch, stalwart Lindsay. How good of you both to rally round this bereft old woman.

(*The others exchange glances.*)

PATRICK: Doesn't she look great?

LINDSAY: Mame, you look marvelous.

VERA (*eying the widow's weeds suspiciously*): How can you tell? Mame, couldn't you have gone to *purple* by now?

LINDSAY: Mame, I haven't seen you since the Huns took Rome. Oh, no, it was when the Bears took Wall Street.

AUNTIE MAME: Oh, Lindsay, that day was nirvana compared with what I've been through since. If only I'd jumped off the Matterhorn after him.

PATRICK (*crossing to the bar*): Now, now, Auntie Mame—
what you need is a good stiff drink.

AUNTIE MAME: No, no, no, Patrick. There is no barbitu-
rate for my grief. I've given up alcohol completely.
I haven't touched a drop since that St. Bernard
brought me back to life. (*She becomes aware of the
dictating machine and the typewriter.*) What's that?

LINDSAY: Well, that's your Dictaphone and this is your
typewriter.

(GOOCH *comes out of hiding and plods flat-footedly
to her place at the desk.* AUNTIE MAME *looks at the
secretary blankly.*)

AUNTIE MAME: And what's *that?*

GOOCH: I'm your "sponge"!

LINDSAY (*clears his throat to spring his surprise*): These are
the tools of your new trade. You're going to write a
book, Mame, and I'm going to publish it.

AUNTIE MAME (*waving away the paraphernalia, including
AGNES*): Oh, Lindsay, don't be ridiculous. The way
I feel, I can hardly read a book, let alone write one.

LINDSAY (*convincingly*): All I want you to do is put your
self on paper. Your memoirs.

PATRICK: Nobody's had a more exciting life than you,
Auntie Mame. Done more things. I think it'd be
terrific.

VERA: And think of all the fascinating people you've
known. Like me.

LINDSAY: And it'll take your mind off things.

AUNTIE MAME (*suspiciously*): Oh, I see—this is some kind of conspiracy.

LINDSAY: No, no—

AUNTIE MAME: Some trumped-up occupational therapy, like leathercraft, or hooking rugs.

LINDSAY: I swear to you, it'll be a fascinating book. Why, it can easily be a best seller. Mame, you'd be doing *me* a favor.

AUNTIE MAME (*starting to pace, intrigued*): My memoirs. My memoirs. Patrick, you forgot my drink.

PATRICK: There's only Southern Comfort.

AUNTIE MAME: Anything, dear, just make it a double. (*She peels off some of the crepe, dumping it in* GOOCH'S *lap.*) What a lovely, lovely idea. I see it in two volumes, don't you, Lindsay? Boxed, like Proust.

LINDSAY: Let's get something to bind first. Remember, Mame, writing isn't easy—it means at least six months of grueling concentration.

AUNTIE MAME (*her eyes lighting up*): Let me see, let me see. (GOOCH *takes her pad and poises her pencil like a female Boswell.*) "Chapter One, Page One!" (GOOCH *writes furiously.*) Well, I'll be damned! This isn't so difficult, Lindsay. (*To* GOOCH, *puzzled.*) What are you writing?

GOOCH (*reading back her shorthand by rote*): "Chapter One, Page One, well, I'll be damned, this isn't so difficult, Lindsay, what are you writing."

VERA: She *is* fast.

PATRICK (*handing the drink to* MAME): Atta girl, Auntie Mame—you're off and running.

AUNTIE MAME (*to* PATRICK): Oh, Patrick, do you really think I should? You heard Lindsay. After all, it'll take up all my time, and I really came home just to be with you.

PATRICK: You can't exactly be with me. No women allowed in the dorm.

AUNTIE MAME: I keep forgetting. You're all grown up now. You don't need me any more. (GOOCH *is still taking down every word in frantic shorthand.* AUNTIE MAME *looks toward* LINDSAY.) How do you turn her off? (*She resumes pacing.*) Now, where was I? The most important thing is to have a good beginning.

VERA : Is she supposed to start right this minute?

LINDSAY: Why don't you wait for your collaborator? He's on his way over here right now.

(*There is a blank pause.*)

AUNTIE MAME: Collaborator?

LINDSAY (*backing water*): Well, after all, you're only an ama—you're not a professional writer, and naturally I thought you'd want as much help as we could . . . (LINDSAY *sees that this is completely the wrong tack. He puts on his most winning and gracious publisher's air.*) Mary Lord Bishop over at my office lined up this young man who's done a great deal of work with women authors, and . . .

AUNTIE MAME (*with smoldering indignation*): You don't trust me to write my own life myself! My God, who else could write it? (*She turns to* VERA *with a hollow laugh.*) He wants to give me a ghost!

LINDSAY: Not a ghost. More of an editor.

AUNTIE MAME: Who? Maxwell Perkins?

LINDSAY: Well, not quite. I haven't met this chap, O'Bannion, myself, but . . .

AUNTIE MAME: What did you say his name was?

LINDSAY: Brian O'Bannion. He's a . . .

AUNTIE MAME: Oh, God, deliver me. I can see him now —one of those beery, loose-mouthed Irish tenors.

LINDSAY: Mary says he's a very good poet. Wrote a volume called *The Wounded Tulip.*

AUNTIE MAME: Probably pansy.

LINDSAY: Now, Mame.

AUNTIE MAME: Do you think I'm going to let some mooneyed versifier mess up my memoirs with a lot of miserable Irish wit? (*The doorbell buzzes.* PATRICK *crosses to the door and opens it. He converses in hushed tones with the visitor.* AUNTIE MAME *rails on against* LINDSAY *and his editorial notions.*) I'll bet you don't give Willa Cather a low-comedy Irishman to tell her how to punctuate! Some funny-paper Jiggs out of Lady Gregory who . . .

PATRICK: Auntie Mame. There's a gentleman to see you. Mr. O'Bannion.

(AUNTIE MAME *looks toward the doorway as* O'BANNION *enters. He is about thirty-five, tall, and very thin. He has a white skin and hair as black as coal— short and very curly. His eyes are turquoise-blue, rimmed with thick, black lashes. He wears a sportcoat of tweedy homespun with big suede patches at the elbows and a dirty trench coat is slung over his shoulder.* O'BANNION *shifts his weight gracefully in the doorway and gives* AUNTIE MAME *a slow, sad smile, parting a fine set of choppers. His intense blue eyes seem to reach out and caress her.*)

O'BANNION (*mellifluously*): Miss Bishop said it might not be amiss if I happened to drop by. (O'BANNION *half closes his eyes.*) You're Mrs. Burnside, of course. I could sense the aura of creative vitality about.

(VERA, LINDSAY, *and* GOOCH *swing their respective gazes slowly from the newcomer to* AUNTIE MAME.)

AUNTIE MAME (*swallowing, a little flustered*): Won't you come in, Mr. O'Bannion? We were just talking about you. (*He comes into the room like a graceful cat, slithering around the furniture with a kind of pelvis movement that is vaguely imitative of an electric eel.* LINDSAY, VERA, *and* GOOCH *watch, fascinated by the crackling chemistry between* O'BANNION *and* AUNTIE MAME.) So awfully kind of you—a really renowned poet—to bother with my childish little scribblings. (*He gives her the old hot-eye again and she clears her throat nervously. As she crosses to him, she takes off her coat, dropping it behind her.*) Tell me, do you think that you and I can ever get any place? (*Quickly.*) With the book, I mean.

(O'BANNION *takes* AUNTIE MAME'S *hand in both of his and turns on that slow, sad smile again.*)

O'BANNION: I feel that you and I are going to create something beautiful!

(The poet draws AUNTIE MAME *closer to him, kissing
her hand. She turns her back to the audience, and we
see that her "widow's weeds" are virtually backless;
and somewhere around the fifth lumbar vertebra
there is a vivid heliotrope flower. The lights fade.)*

Again the pinwheel projection spins on the semi-transparent traveler, suggesting a passage of time. In the darkness we hear an ancient Gaelic lullaby, sung touchingly by unseen male voices.

VOICES (*off stage; singing*):

"Tu ra loora lay,
A loora lay,
A toora loora lay;
Tu ra loora lay,
A loora lay,
A toora loora lay."

The lights bleed through the traveler, which is drawn off and reveals:

The Beekman Place apartment—refurnished and refurbished as a literary atelier. The wall panels have been reversed, to become impressive bookcases. A bust of Dickens adorns the niche by the spiral staircase. BRIAN O'BANNION *reclines on a leathery love seat.*

*To say he has made himself at home is a gross under-
statement; he is wearing a lush quilted dressing gown
and lounges with half-closed eyes, one forearm dramatically crooked over his meditative forehead.*

AGNES GOOCH *sits like a flat-chested owl at her typewriter. Intensely she pounds away at a manuscript,
the stethoscope of a Dictaphone dangling from her
ears. Apparently what she hears stirs the spirit of
Proserpina in her otherwise vacuous vitals. Occasionally a little "coo" of excitement escapes her lips,
prompted by what is coming through the earphones.
Her eyes sparkle, and she types furiously with vicari-
ous delight.*

O'BANNION (*annoyed*): Please, please—Miss Gooch! How
can I court the Muse with all that clackety-clackety?

GOOCH: I'm just taking off what Mrs. Burnside dictated.
(O'BANNION *makes a deprecating gesture, waving aside
anything that* AUNTIE MAME *has dictated as unimportant.*) But everything Mrs. Burnside dictates is so
wonderful, it makes me all goose pimply. Why, when
I listen to all the things she's done, and think of all
the things I haven't done, I just want to go out and
start trying everything and seeing everything and being everything—just like she has!

O'BANNION: I'm not sure the human race is ready for this
book. (*Grandly.*) But it is *I* who shall clothe the
naked incidents in poetry and symbolism. (*He glances
at his watch and calls off insolently.*) Norah! Ito! It's
time for my nectar.

(NORAH *enters from the kitchen, her hands on her hips and sizing up* O'BANNION.)

NORAH: What's that of yours it's time for, Your Majesty?

O'BANNION: My nectar, my nectar!

NORAH (*sarcastically*): In exactly what part of Ireland is it, me bucko, where you drink "nectar"?

O'BANNION (*laying it on, airily*): I come from that part of the Green Isle that has no latitude, nor longitude, and the leprechauns play in the twilight mist . . .

NORAH: You know, you're just about four bricks short of a full load! (*She goes off disgustedly.*)

(*The telephone rings and* AGNES *answers it.*)

GOOCH (*into phone*): Mrs. Burnside's residence. No, she isn't here—she's out on the moors. (*Pause.*) The moors. (*She listens again.*) Maybe you'd better talk to Mr. O'Bannion. (GOOCH *gets up from her desk and carries the telephone on a long cord to the recumbent* O'BANNION.) It's that Mr. M. Lindsay Woolsey. He says it's important.

(*Grandly* O'BANNION *takes the telephone from the servile secretary, who trembles with excitement the instant their hands brush.*)

O'BANNION (*into phone*): O'Bannion here. How are you, Lindsay? (*He listens.*) The moors? Oh, that's what we call the terrace where I send her to meditate when the fog is crawling up from the Queensborough Bridge. (*He listens again.*) I can't put her on, but I'll be happy to give her another message. (*This probably nettles* LINDSAY, *but* O'BANNION *continues with his attitude of bland mastery of the situation.*) I'll tell her. But of course she'll be at your party tonight— *I'm* bringing her. Goldwyn? Samuel Goldwyn? (*He listens; this boy can smell a buck.*) Well, if he's interested, he'll have to buy our book sight unseen! (*He hangs up.*)

(AUNTIE MAME *enters, looking like a Brontë with a long plaid muffler around her throat.*)

AUNTIE MAME: Oh, how the air of the moors releases the creative juices in the brain. Suddenly the fog lifted —and there was Welfare Island, looking for all the world like one magnificent peat bog.

O'BANNION (*eagerly*): Alana, Samuel Goldwyn's coming to the party tonight. And we're to be at Lindsay's a half hour early to tell him the story.

AUNTIE MAME: Dear Lindsay! How good of him. Goldwyn's perfect for my story. After all, it *is* the American *Wuthering Heights*.

(GOOCH *comes forward, apologizing for living. In one hand she has a stack of manuscript as thick as the New York telephone directory, and in the other hand she has two pages.*)

GOOCH (*indicating the thick sheaf of pages*): Here's what you dictated, Mrs. Burnside . . . (*And indicating the two sheets.*) . . . and here's what Mr. O'Bannion edited.

AUNTIE MAME: Oh. Thank you, Agnes. Now Mr. O'Bannion and I are going to work for a little bit. Why don't you do whatever it is you *do* do to relax?

GOOCH: Oh, thank you, Mrs. Burnside. I think I'll just fix myself a Dr. Pepper.

(GOOCH *takes a glass from the bar and goes off to the kitchen. She looks moon-eyed at* O'BANNION *as she exits.*

The moment she is gone, O'BANNION *tries to nuzzle* AUNTIE MAME, *but deftly she slips away from his embrace.*)

O'BANNION: You glorious creature!

AUNTIE MAME: Brian—please—we're supposed to be working.

O'BANNION: Every time I come within ten feet of you, you reject me. How can we make music, until our lutes are in tune?

AUNTIE MAME: Well, after we finish the book, we can tune our lutes.

O'BANNION: We're not collaborating in the fullest sense of the word. (*Amorously.*) Alana, collaborate with me!

AUNTIE MAME: Brian, really!

O'BANNION: You're a block of ice, and we're supposed to be writing of burning passion and hot blood.

AUNTIE MAME: But I'm only eleven years of age in this part of the book.

O'BANNION: But *mature*—mature for eleven!

AUNTIE MAME: Brian, we've got to get to work.

O'BANNION (*sighs*): All right, slave driver. Where were we?

(AUNTIE MAME, *relieved, examines the two pages that are the total of* O'BANNION's *editing.*)

AUNTIE MAME: Still on Chapter Two. It's not going very fast, is it? It took us a month and a half on Chapter One.

O'BANNION: But what a chapter!

AUNTIE MAME: What a month and a half. (*Fending him off.*) Please, Brian, I cannot concentrate when you're doing things like that.

O'BANNION: Sorceress!

AUNTIE MAME: Besides, it takes Agnes no time at all to knock off a Dr. Pepper. (*Wishing the whole thing were over.*) How long do you think it's going to take us to finish the book?

O'BANNION: Flaubert spent thirteen years on *Madame Bovary*.

AUNTIE MAME: How did she stand it?

O'BANNION: Read me our last sentence.

(AUNTIE MAME *reaches for the top page on the thick stack of manuscript, and reads.*)

AUNTIE MAME (*reading*): "My puberty in Buffalo was drab."

O'BANNION: No, no! It has no majesty! "Drab" is such a drab word.

AUNTIE MAME: How right you are, Brian. It has no afflatus. (GOOCH *enters from the kitchen, pouring a Dr. Pepper into a highball glass.* AUNTIE MAME *looks at her and gets an idea.*) What about "bleak"?

O'BANNION (*testing it*): Bleak . . . bleak! How bleak was

my puberty! Bleak Buffalo. Hear how those two words cling to each other—like a man and a woman, locked in each other's arms! Listen to the words sing!

GOOCH (*enraptured*): How bleak was my puberty!

(AUNTIE MAME *glares at* GOOCH, *who melts away into the kitchen.*)

GOOCH: I'm sorry.

(*As soon as* GOOCH *is out of sight,* O'BANNION *goes to work again, kissing* AUNTIE MAME *helter-skelter.*)

O'BANNION: "Bleak." Oh, God, let me caress that talent! Where is it hidden, that germ of genius, *where* is it?

AUNTIE MAME: Brian, please—(*She glances at the page of edited manuscript.*) I'm worried about something. Coccamaura. I wonder if the general public is going to understand all this symbolism. (*She reads.*) "Like an echo from the caves of Coccamaura, I came forth whilst Deirdre wept cool tears." Wouldn't it be simpler to say, "On the day I was born, it rained in Buffalo"?

O'BANNION: Drab, drab, drab!

AUNTIE MAME: It's drab, but it's clear.

O'BANNION: Clarity! How beauty is obscured by clarity.

AUNTIE MAME: All right, Brian, just what is it you want to say?

O'BANNION (*fumbling*): Well, it's quite obvious—(*Suddenly he makes an extravagant gesture.*) We're drying up! We need inspiration! Get out the Yeats, the Synge, the Joyce! It's poetry time!

AUNTIE MAME (*wearily*): Again??? (AUNTIE MAME *takes a*

thin volume from the table. Although she is bored with this poetry ritual, she accepts it as a part of the eccentric trappings of authorship. Resignedly she slips to the floor with O'BANNION *and they lie head to head, their feet extending in opposite directions. With dutiful concentration she begins to read.)*
"The lyre and lute
Are mute, are mute,
And gray is the grave where my lover lies;
Where my lover lies,
Where my lover lies,
Mute, mute, mute."

(GOOCH *comes in, stepping over them.)*

GOOCH: I rinsed out the glass.

AUNTIE MAME: Aren't you neat, Agnes.

(GOOCH *plods back into the kitchen.)*

O'BANNION: Glorious! Glorious! More! More!

(AUNTIE MAME *turns to another poem.* PATRICK *appears in the hallway and lets himself in.*

AUNTIE MAME *and* O'BANNION *are so wrapped up in their "work" that they do not hear the sound of* PATRICK *coming in. She reads.)*

AUNTIE MAME: "Bright bleeds the blood of the broken rose,
And my loins leap up to utter passion's feckless cry.
My loins cry out for thee,
O Love!
O Love!—"

(O'BANNION *has been acting out the imagery on* AUNTIE MAME'S *neck and ear;* PATRICK *clears his throat.*)

Oh, hush, Agnes.

PATRICK (*coolly*): Auntie Mame—

(AUNTIE MAME *and* O'BANNION *spring up from the floor.* AUNTIE MAME *is a little flustered.*)

AUNTIE MAME: Why, Patrick—what are you doing home from school?

PATRICK: I had something very important I wanted to talk with you about—but if you're busy . . .

AUNTIE MAME (*covering quickly*): Oh, Brian and I were just working—on the book.

PATRICK: I'll bet that's going to be some book.

AUNTIE MAME: This is my nephew, Patrick; this is my collaborator, Mr. Brian O'Bannion.

(*The two nod to each other with the cordiality of Ben Gurion encountering Nasser.*)

PATRICK (*glumly*): We've met. Auntie Mame, I wonder if I could talk to you a little bit—alone. It's rather personal—and rather important.

AUNTIE MAME: Why, of course, my dear. If you don't mind, Brian—?

(O'BANNION, *somewhat wounded, decides to make an exit.*)

O'BANNION (*starting up the staircase*): It's quite all right. I was just going up to my room—to change. (*Raising his voice.*) Pay no attention to me. Don't anybody pay any attention to me at all! (*He exits grandly up the stairs.*)

PATRICK: To his *room!* Is he *living* here?

AUNTIE MAME: Why, of course, darling. There was nobody in the sculpture room. And since we're working together literally day and night—so to speak . . .

PATRICK (*primly*): It looks very cozy.

AUNTIE MAME: For a moment there you sounded exactly like somebody from the Knickerbocker Bank.

PATRICK: Please get O'Bannion out of here. Right away.

AUNTIE MAME: I beg your pardon?

PATRICK: I don't want him in this house.

AUNTIE MAME: Aren't you taking a rather imperious tone? Mr. O'Bannion is my colleague.

PATRICK: Colleague, my foot! Gloria would never understand that you and this Irish phoney are . . .

AUNTIE MAME: Gloria? Who's Gloria?

(PATRICK *takes a deep breath.*)

PATRICK: Auntie Mame, listen to me. (*He takes her shoulders.*) I've met a girl. I've been going with her for several months.

AUNTIE MAME: Oh?

PATRICK: She's—well, she's a very special girl. I guess I should have told you about her before. I *would* have, but I knew you were all tied up with your book and . . . (*Significantly.*) . . . everything. And until now it wasn't really definite.

AUNTIE MAME: What's definite now?

PATRICK: Gloria's *the* girl, that's what's definite. And you're going to meet her. Tonight.

AUNTIE MAME: I hope you didn't leave her sitting in the car.

PATRICK: I dropped her off at her girl friend's. Bunny Bixler's on Park Avenue. She wanted to get spruced up before she met you.

AUNTIE MAME (*nervously*): Well—I'd better do some sprucing up of my own.

PATRICK (*starting toward the door*): I'll bring Gloria back in about ten or fifteen minutes, okay?

AUNTIE MAME (*a little flustered*): I'll have my face all organized.

(*From off, we hear* O'BANNION'S *voice at the top of the stairs.*)

O'BANNION (*calling*): Mame, where did Ito hide my white tie?

(PATRICK *stops dead in his tracks, pointing his finger toward the sound of the voice.*)

PATRICK: Wait a minute. If *he's* still in the house, I'm not going to bring Gloria back here.

AUNTIE MAME: May I inquire why?

PATRICK: Gloria happens to be a very sensitive and well-brought-up girl. And I don't want you flaunting your new flames and your old peccadilloes in front of her.

AUNTIE MAME (*freezing*): Then why bring her here at all?

PATRICK (*getting angry himself*): You want to know the truth? I've been trying to avoid it. But she wanted to meet you.

AUNTIE MAME: So you just dropped by to make sure I was all scrubbed up and presentable for inspection! Is that it?

PATRICK (*suffering*): Now, Auntie Mame. (*Pleading.*) Just for five minutes tonight will you try to act like a normal human being? Then I won't make any more demands on you. Gloria's from good stock—and she just doesn't have to know about all your airy-fairy friends from Fire Island; or your Irish friend up-stairs. I'd just rather my little Glory didn't know about a lot of things that ordinary mortals simply don't have to know about.

(*There is a deathly pause.*)

AUNTIE MAME (*with quiet intensity*): Should she know that I think you've turned into one of the most beastly, bourgeois, babbitty little snobs on the Eastern seaboard—or will you be able to make that *quite* clear, without any help from me?

(*This is the first time in* PATRICK'S *entire life that* AUNTIE MAME *has really let him have it with both barrels. He is stunned. He looks at her for a moment, then turns on his heels and starts out.*)

PATRICK: All right. Just forget about the whole thing.

(AUNTIE MAME *realizes it would be fatal to let him go out in this mood.*)

AUNTIE MAME: Patrick—bring your girl here. I won't let her get the wrong impression, I promise.

(*They look at each other.*)

PATRICK (*with a warm smile*): Thanks, Auntie Mame. (*He goes off.*)

(AUNTIE MAME *begins to pace, chewing on the knuckle of her index finger. From upstairs we hear* O'BANNION'S *untrained Irish baritone singing, "I'll Take You Home Again, Kathleen." At this sound,* AUNTIE MAME *really looks worried: How is she going to get him out of here?*)

AUNTIE MAME (*calling up the stairs*): Brian . . .

(O'BANNION *breaks off in midsong and appears at the head of the stairs in full-dress shirt and trousers—but no tie or coat yet.*)

O'BANNION (*from the head of the stairs*): Yes, Alana? Why aren't you getting dressed? We can't keep the Goldwyns waiting.

AUNTIE MAME (*with difficulty*): Would you mind awfully if I didn't go to the party with you tonight?

O'BANNION (*affronted*): You want me to go *alone?* I wouldn't think of it!

AUNTIE MAME: But—something came up . . .

O'BANNION (*imperiously*): Hurry and get dressed, Alana. I'm *not* goin' to that party alone! (*He turns on his heel and goes back into his upstairs bedroom.*

GOOCH *plods out of the kitchen and whines at* AUNTIE MAME.)

GOOCH: Mrs. Burnside, if there's nothing else you wanted me for, I just thought I'd turn in.

AUNTIE MAME: Agnes, I wonder—(AUNTIE MAME *starts pacing around* GOOCH.)

GOOCH (*getting nervous at* AUNTIE MAME'S *perusal*): Mrs. Burnside, is anything wrong?

AUNTIE MAME: Agnes! You're coming out.

GOOCH (*clutching the sides of her dress*): Where?

AUNTIE MAME (*yanking off* GOOCH'S *glasses*): Why, Agnes, you have lovely eyes. Take those glasses off and leave them off *forever*.

GOOCH: But I can't see anything out of my right eye.

AUNTIE MAME: Then look out of the left one. (AUNTIE MAME *points to* GOOCH'S *shoes*.) What do you call *those* things?

GOOCH: Orthopedic oxfords.

AUNTIE MAME: Kick 'em off! (GOOCH, *baffled, complies.* AUNTIE MAME *pulls her dress tight around the midriff*.) My goodness, Agnes—you *do* have a bust. Where on earth have you been hiding it all these months?

GOOCH (*getting worried*): Mrs. Burnside—

AUNTIE MAME (*positively*): Take off your clothes.

GOOCH (*with a proper little gasp*): Mrs. Burnside! There's a man in the house!

AUNTIE MAME: Don't be a goose, Agnes, get these clothes off and keep them off. (GOOCH *peels out of her clothes and stands trembling in a shapeless white slip.* MAME *calls off.*) Norah! Ito! Come on in here, we've got some work to do!

(NORAH *and* ITO *hurry in from the kitchen.*)

GOOCH (*cringing*): I don't have a very clear picture of what's going on.

AUNTIE MAME (*briskly*): Agnes, I'm sending you to that party tonight with Mr. O'Bannion.

(GOOCH *looks thunderstruck and begins to get the shakes.*)

GOOCH: Oh, I couldn't. I'm too nervous.

(AUNTIE MAME *strides to the bar and pours a stiff slug of Irish whisky for* GOOCH.)

AUNTIE MAME: This'll calm you down.

GOOCH: But spirits do the most terrible thing to me. I'm not the same girl.

AUNTIE MAME: What's wrong with that? (*She forces the jigger on* GOOCH. *The secretary starts to drink, then hesitates.*)

GOOCH: Will it mix with Dr. Pepper?

AUNTIE MAME (*emphatically*): He'll love it. Drink! (GOOCH *drinks. Before the liquor hits bottom,* AUNTIE MAME *is slapping* GOOCH's *cheeks.*) Oh, Agnes, for God's sake, close your pores! We really should do something about that skin. A good physic would work wonders, but I guess it's too late in the day to start that. (*She turns crisply to the servants.*) Norah, go upstairs, drag out that sexy Patou velvet! Ito, get out all my cosmetics: the face creams, the lipsticks, the eyebrow pencils!

(ITO *scampers up the stairs delightedly.*)

ITO: You see, me be Charlie of the Ritz!

(AUNTIE MAME *starts to drag* GOOCH *up the stairs, but* GOOCH *hangs back, holding onto the banister.*)

GOOCH (*a coward to the core*): Mrs. Burnside, I think I know what you want me to do, and I'm not a bit sure I want to do it!

AUNTIE MAME: Agnes, where's your *spine?* Here you've been taking my dictation all these weeks, and you don't get the message of my book! *Live!—That's* the message!

GOOCH (*still hanging back, as if she didn't know what the word meant*): Live?

AUNTIE MAME: Yes! Life is a banquet, and most poor sons-of-bitches are *starving* to death! Live!

(*Intoxicated, partly by the liquor, partly by* AUNTIE MAME'S *enthusiasm,* GOOCH *decides to let herself go.*)

GOOCH (*hypnotized*): Live! Live! Live!

(*The lights fade.*)

The Beekman Place apartment, a half hour later.

As the lights come up, the room is empty. Then ITO *scampers down the spiral stairs, giggling giddily. He disappears into the kitchen.*

Next NORAH *hurries down the stairs, gathering up some of* GOOCH's *discarded clothing.*

NORAH (*muttering*): The whole house has gone nuts! (*Shaking her head as she goes off.*) She'll never make a silk purse out of *that* sow's ear!

(*Now* AUNTIE MAME *appears at the head of the stairs. She turns back as* GOOCH *calls to her from off.*)

GOOCH'S VOICE (*calling from off*): Mrs. Burnside, I can't *breathe!*

AUNTIE MAME: Fine! If you can breathe, it isn't tight enough. (AUNTIE MAME *starts down the stairs, carrying a fur wrap. She looks at her watch. Under her breath.*) Oh, God.

(*Glancing nervously toward the outside door, she takes several glasses toward the bar, straightening up for* GLORIA'S *imminent arrival. In the manner of a grand duke,* O'BANNION *comes down the stairs in his full-dress regalia.*)

O'BANNION (*startled*): And why aren't you ready?

AUNTIE MAME (*turning to face* O'BANNION): Now, Brian, you're going to have to understand. I'm not going to the party tonight.

O'BANNION (*splenetically*): Then *I'm* not going either! (*Stamping his foot.*) I'm not, I'm not, I'm *not!*

AUNTIE MAME: You can use the Dusenberg. And I've got a date for you!

O'BANNION: Who? (*Slightly mollified.*) Vera?

AUNTIE MAME: Certainly not. You couldn't trust Vera. (*Going to the foot of the stairs and calling up.*) Agnes—?

O'BANNION: Agnes! You certainly can't expect me to be seen at a fashionable party with that—(*Haughtily.*) Would you ask Toscanini to lead a harmonica band? I'm staying right here!

AUNTIE MAME: Now, Brian.

O'BANNION: You don't appreciate me. I'm a minstrel without a lute—

AUNTIE MAME: Not those lutes again.

O'BANNION (*throwing himself on the sofa and kicking his heels like a petulant infant*): I won't take Agnes to the party! I won't, I won't, I won't, I won't!

(GOOCH *starts down the stairs.*)

AUNTIE MAME (*coaching*): Head up! Shoulders back! Tummy in! That's right! Tonight you're the Queen of Rumania!

(GOOCH *looks almost regal.* O'BANNION'S *jaw drops.*)

O'BANNION: Well! (O'BANNION *gives her the old hot-eye; then offers* GOOCH *his arm, and she takes it.*)

GOOCH (*transported*): Hotcha!

(*In the outer hallway,* PATRICK *and* GLORIA *appear.* PATRICK *starts to use his key to let himself in, then thinks better of it and presses the door buzzer.* AUNTIE MAME *jumps.*)

AUNTIE MAME: Quick, Brian. Hang those furs on the Gooch. Hurry! (*She hesitates for a moment, then crosses to the door with some misgivings. She opens the door and greets* PATRICK *and* GLORIA.)

PATRICK (*as if he were presenting the Kimberly diamond*): Auntie Mame, this is Gloria. Gloria Upson. And this is my Auntie Mame. Mrs. Burnside.

GLORIA (*extending a limp hand*): I can't tell you how pleased I am to make your acquaintance.

(GLORIA *is lovely, tanned, pleasant, but without real warmth. There is something wrong with this girl— you can't quite put your finger on it—a kind of ersatz composure, a mail-order chic. When she talks, there seems to be novocain in her upper lip.*)

AUNTIE MAME: Come in, children, come in. There are some friends here I want you to meet.

PATRICK (*bristling*): Auntie Mame, you promised—

(*But* AUNTIE MAME *is completely composed as she ushers them into the living room.*)

AUNTIE MAME: This is my secretary, Miss Gooch. My good right hand, my Alice B. Toklas, you might say. (*With an appropriate gesture.*) This is Miss Upson, and my nephew Patrick.

(GOOCH's *eyes light up at the sight of* PATRICK.)

GOOCH: Oh, can this be the helpless little infant you found in a basket on your doorstep?

AUNTIE MAME (*indicating the resplendent* O'BANNION): And this is Agnes' *date.* What's your boy friend's name, Agnes? O'Bannion, wasn't it?

(PATRICK *breathes a sigh of relief at his aunt's deft recovery.*)

O'BANNION (*curtly*): We'll be on our way. Good night.

GLORIA: I can't tell you how pleased I am to have made your acquaintance, Mr. O'Bannion. (*Turning to* GOOCH.) And Miss Toklas.

(O'BANNION *and* GOOCH *go out.*)

AUNTIE MAME (*taking* GLORIA's *hands*): Patrick says you're very special to him; that means you're very special to me, too.

GLORIA (*looking about, vacuously*): My! What a stunning apartment. Don't tell me you've read all these books, Mrs. Burnside!

AUNTIE MAME: Well, not all of them. Do sit down, dear. Can I get you something? A cognac, or a Drambuie—

PATRICK: Would you like another hot chocolate, honey?

GLORIA: Oh, not a *thing*. On our way to Bunny's, Patrick and I just stuffed ourselves at Howard Johnson's. (GLORIA *laughs musically*.) And do you know what your silly nephew did? He talked French to the waiter. Imagine anybody talking French to a waiter at a Howard Johnson's! (*She nudges him playfully*.) Show-off!

AUNTIE MAME: If nobody minds, I think *I'll* have something. (*She pours herself a brandy; her face is troubled by her first appraisal of the girl—but she's determined to keep an open mind*.) You're at school, dear?

GLORIA: I'm a Sweetbriar girl.

AUNTIE MAME: How did you get that lovely tan so early in spring?

GLORIA: Oh, I played hookey for a couple of weeks. Mums and Daddums and I went down to our place in Fort Lauderdale. We have a place in Fort Lauderdale.

PATRICK: While she was gone, it was the longest two weeks in my life. And yet—it's the funniest thing, Auntie Mame—when Gloria and I are together, we don't really *do* much of anything. I mean, we don't even talk—I'm just so busy staring at her.

GLORIA: Silly.

AUNTIE MAME: Have you chosen your major yet, dear?

GLORIA (*blankly*): Chosen my major?

AUNTIE MAME: What courses are you taking at college?

GLORIA: Oh, just a general sort of liberal arts thing. You know, English Lit and like that. Sweetbriar's top-hole. Really top-hole.

AUNTIE MAME: How did you two ever get acquainted?

GLORIA: Oh, Uncle Dwight introduced us.

AUNTIE MAME: Uncle Dwight?

PATRICK: That's Mr. Babcock.

AUNTIE MAME: Oh, yes.

GLORIA: He's not really my uncle. But he's been a real close friend of the family ever since I was a little girl with braces on my teeth.

AUNTIE MAME: Well, any time you want to take your old aunt into the family circle, just let me know. . . .

PATRICK: Oh, we don't want to bother you with a lot of family stuff.

GLORIA: Naturally, we'll expect you at the wedding.

AUNTIE MAME (*pale*): The wedding?

PATRICK: I told you it was definite, Auntie Mame.

GLORIA: We've decided on a September wedding. It's lovely, just lovely then at the Church of the Heavenly Rest—that's right near our place in Mountebank.

AUNTIE MAME: September. Dear me. Tell me—just where is Mountebank?

GLORIA: Right above Darien. You'll love it. It's the most restricted community in our part of Connecticut.

AUNTIE MAME: I'll get a blood test.

(PATRICK *knows a storm cloud when he sees one, and he's determined to get his girl out before the downpour.*)

PATRICK: If we hurry, we could still catch the last couple of dances at the country club.

AUNTIE MAME: I hate to have you rush off.

(*But* GLORIA *doesn't care about sticking around here; she smiles synthetically and stiff-arms a handshake.*)

GLORIA: I can't tell you how pleased I am to have made your acquaintance.

PATRICK (*halfway to the door*): I'll drop you a note and let you know what's happening.

AUNTIE MAME: Do that!

(GLORIA *goes out,* PATRICK *turns.*)

PATRICK (*lowering his voice*): Isn't she a dream?

AUNTIE MAME: Oh, yes—yes, she is. . . . Did I pass inspection?

PATRICK: You were great, Auntie Mame. Really top-hole.

(PATRICK *goes off.* AUNTIE MAME *stands alone, a little dazed—and not at all sure that what has just happened has really happened.*)

AUNTIE MAME (*with a semi-bitter bemusement*): Why did I ever buy him those long pants?

(*The lights fade.*)

*An upstairs hallway, early morning of the following
day. The traveler has been drawn and the action takes
place in one.*

NORAH *and* ITO *cross from opposite sides of the stage.*
ITO *is wearing a chauffeur's uniform;* NORAH *is carrying a breakfast tray containing juice and a raw egg.*

ITO (*confused*): Missy say go to garage, get Dusenberg—
we drive to Connecticut today—very important. I go
to garage. No Dusenberg.

NORAH: And it's His Majesty's breakfast I've got here.
Only there's not a smell of that O'Bannion in the
place. You suppose he's gone for good, God bless the
day?

ITO: Me no know what to do. Got road map to Mountebank. Got uniform. No Dusenberg.

NORAH: That Mr. Lindsay always has a car or two. (*She
hands* ITO *the egg cup.*) The glorious thing is that
O'Bannion's gone. You can have his raw egg. I'll
drink his nectar.

(*But they stop abruptly as* GOOCH *staggers on. The strap of her evening dress is askew, her hair is tangled, and she has a definite "out-all-night" air about her.*)

ITO: What happen, Missy Gooch?

GOOCH: I *lived!*

NORAH: What kind of a party was that?

GOOCH: Oh, we never got to that party. Brian said he was going to take me for a drive. But we parked.

ITO: Where Dusenberg now, Missy Gooch?

GOOCH: Brian dropped me off here—and said he was driving due west. (*Looks around, panicky.*) Where's Mrs. Burnside?

ITO: She put on face—get ready for trip to Connecticut.

GOOCH: I've got to see her before she goes.

NORAH: Is anything wrong, Miss Gooch?

GOOCH: I did just what she told me. I lived! I've got to find out what to do *now!!!*

(ITO *and* NORAH *look at each other significantly as* GOOCH *shuffles off. The lights fade.*)

The patio of the Upsons' home in Mountebank. Late afternoon. Before the lights come up, the prattle of extroverted chickadees informs us that we have reached the apotheosis of exurbia. The sunlight of a late spring afternoon slants across the little flagstone heaven where the UPSONS *take their ease.* MR. UPSON *is carrying out the bar stools—Early American; and* MRS. UPSON *enters with a tray of hors d'oeuvres—also Early American. The* UPSONS *are a hearty, well-padded couple, enormously pleased with themselves and their way of life. The decor includes a precious birdhouse and a cunning wagonwheel concealing an artful gap in the whitewashed fence.*

MRS. UPSON: Well, I just think it's a very good match for our little Gloria, that's what *I* think. (MRS. UPSON *is fluttering nervously about, prettying up the patio. She is a rosy, flaccid woman who thinks Walter Lippmann makes tea.* MR. UPSON *is loud and square as the basement of a Masonic temple. He thinks Walter Lippmann is a Socialist.*)

MR. UPSON (*lifting up his paraphernalia on the bar*): I still can't see why Dwight didn't want us to meet the aunt.

MRS. UPSON: I guess we never would have if she hadn't phoned. I thought it was only my duty to ask her to buzz up here. Besides, I was dying to get a look at her.

MR. UPSON: Where is she now?

MRS. UPSON: She's up in the guest room changing again.

MR. UPSON: She certainly brought enough clothes.

MRS. UPSON: And they're expensive ones, Claude; I looked at the labels.

MR. UPSON: Why, I'll bet she's even better fixed than Dwight figured.

(MRS. UPSON *purses her lips, a little worried.*)

MRS. UPSON: I hope it's all right to have the cocktail hour here on the patio. I don't want her to think we live like gypsies.

MR. UPSON: You show me a gypsy that lives like we do.

(*He chortles with self-satisfaction.*)

MRS. UPSON: Now, Claude Upson, you be *genteel* in front of Mrs. Burnside!

MR. UPSON (*belligerently*): God damn it, I'm *always* genteel!

(*From inside the house, we hear* AUNTIE MAME *call out in her most Connecticut manner.*)

AUNTIE MAME'S VOICE (*from off*): Yoo-hoo!

MRS. UPSON: Oh, that must be she. (*She raises her voice.*) We're out here on the patio, Mrs. Burnside.

(AUNTIE MAME, *stunningly dressed for spring-in-the-*

country, starts through the doorway onto the patio, but suddenly loses footing.)

AUNTIE MAME: Oops! (*The* UPSONS *react with concern.*) Oh dear—I'm always tripping over that *adorable* little hooked rug.

MRS. UPSON: Do be careful; we'd feel awful if you had an accident.

MR. UPSON (*jovially*): Don't you worry. I've got plenty of personal liability insurance.

AUNTIE MAME (*blithely*): Well, then, let's bring on more hooked rugs!

MR. UPSON: Now, there's one thing we oughta know right off. You *do* take a little nip now and then?

AUNTIE MAME (*smiling prettily*): On festive occasions.

MR. UPSON (*blandly*): Good, I'll have an Upson daiquiri ready in a minute.

(AUNTIE MAME *would rather have vermouth and Castoria, but she indicates her pleasure at the prospect.*)

AUNTIE MAME (*glancing around the patio*): Oh, Mrs. Upson, I can't get over how much thought you've given every detail of your house.

MRS. UPSON: We've done everything we could to make it seem like a little bit of authentic colonial America.

AUNTIE MAME: And how well you've succeeded! Those adorable miniatures in the powder room of John Quincy Adams.

MRS. UPSON: Well, I said to the decorator from Altman's—

AUNTIE MAME: Altman's? I would have said Sloane's. Solid Sloane's!

MRS. UPSON (*giggling*): Don't you have an *eye*, though. *Downstairs* is Sloane's. Upstairs is Altman's!

MR. UPSON (*looking up from his bar chores*): I'll bet you didn't notice our signpost out by the driveway . . . ?

AUNTIE MAME: But I *did!* I did! What a divine name you've chosen for your place. (*Trying to recall.*) "Upson . . ."

UPSONS (*together*): "Downs!"

AUNTIE MAME: I'll bet *you* thought that up, Mrs. Upson.

MRS. UPSON: Oh, no. It was Claude. I'm just a homebody. Claude's the clever one. (MR. UPSON *laughs.*) I'm so delighted to see we have the same tastes. I know you're just going to adore the wedding we've planned for the children.

AUNTIE MAME (*wetting her lips*): Now, about the wedding. Don't you think, Mrs. Upson, that . . .

MR. UPSON: Hold it! Hold it! Let's forget the last names right off. After all, we're practically family, aren't we? I just want to be plain Claude.

MRS. UPSON: And I'm Doris.

AUNTIE MAME: "Doris." I've always loved the name of Doris. Not too coy and not too chic. Sort of bittersweet.

MR. UPSON: What do we call you?

AUNTIE MAME: All my intimate friends call me just plain Mame.

MRS. UPSON: How lovely. (*Trying to get on* AUNTIE MAME's *level.*) Old-fashioned—and yet modern, too. Mamie.

AUNTIE MAME (*correcting*): Mame.

MR. UPSON (*pouring a daiquiri and handing it to her*): Well, Mamie old girl, here's your poison. I make my daiquiris with a secret ingredient I learned from this native down in Havana, Cuba. You'll never guess what the secret ingredient is—but I'll say *this* much. There's no sugar in a Claude Upson daiquiri.

(*She sips it.*)

AUNTIE MAME: And yet it's so *sweet*. What *ever* do you use? Chocolate ice cream?

MR. UPSON (*guffawing*): Sa-a-y, that's rich. Did you hear that, Doris? Chocolate ice cream. (*He puts a bearlike hand on* AUNTIE MAME'S *shoulder.*) Since we're practically relatives, I'm going to let you in on my little secret, *honey.*

AUNTIE MAME: I beg your pardon?

MR. UPSON: Strained honey—that's the secret ingredient. (*He chortles.*) Of course, I use quite a little rum, too!

(MAME *points playfully into her glass and in a hail-fellow-well-met mood.*

MRS. UPSON *comes over with a tray of canapés.*)

MRS. UPSON: Now, I made these especially for you, dear.

AUNTIE MAME (*taking a canapé*): Don't they look delicious, though. Mm-m-m-mm-mm-*mm!* (*She takes a bite.*) What *are* they?

MRS. UPSON: Well, I take two cans of tuna fish and put them through the meat grinder, then add clam juice and peanut butter. It's a recipe I cut out of the *Ladies Home Journal.* (*She proffers the other tray.*)

These others are just plain jack cheese and chutney. (MRS. UPSON *steers* AUNTIE MAME *to a bench. Surreptitiously,* MAME *tosses the hors d'oeuvre over the patio wall.*) Now, sit you down right here, Mamie. There's something *special* I have to show you. (*She pulls out a photo album.*)

AUNTIE MAME (*gleefully*): Baby pictures. Of Gloria?

MRS. UPSON: Oh, the whole family, more or less.

(*They start to leaf through the album.*)

AUNTIE MAME (*pointing to one snap*): On a bear rug! Isn't that precious?

(MAME *tosses her drink over her shoulder when* MRS. UPSON *isn't looking.*)

MRS. UPSON (*giggling*): Better not ever let Patrick see *that* one! That's Miss Tuthill—little Glory's first schoolteacher. I think the light was hurting her eyes. (*She turns another page.*) And here's Gloria when she was a flower girl at Muriel Puce's wedding.

AUNTIE MAME: What's she eating?

MRS. UPSON: Oh, those are the braces on her teeth.

MR. UPSON: All right, all right—that's enough of the girly-girly talk. I figure while we've got Mamie here, we oughta tell her what the plans are. (*He sits beside* MAME, *his fat paw around her shoulder.*)

AUNTIE MAME: Plans?

MR. UPSON: For Patrick's career. Dwight Babcock and I have it all worked out. He came to me, and he said "Claude"—he always calls me Claude—

MRS. UPSON (*confidentially to* AUNTIE MAME, *crowding her*

from the opposite side): When they're together, it's "Dwight and Claude, Claude and Dwight"—that's all you hear.

MR. UPSON: Yup! Yup! Yup! Now, when the kiddies get back from their honeymoon, I want Patrick to take his choice. With my connections, I can slip him into a berth on Madison Avenue or a seat on the Stock Exchange.

AUNTIE MAME: A seat *and* a berth!—(MAME *practically bumps noses with* MRS. UPSON. MR. UPSON *notices her glass is empty.*)

MR. UPSON: Say, you're a fast drinker, Mamie! But don't you worry—I made plenty.

MAME: Oh, I don't think—

(UPSON *takes her glass and crosses to the bar.*)

MRS. UPSON: You don't happen to like gin, do you, Mamie?

AUNTIE MAME (*whispers*): I adore it.

MRS. UPSON: After dinner, I'll get the cards and we'll have a little game.

(UPSON *returns with another daiquiri.*)

MR. UPSON: Now, we come to the problem of what to give the kiddies for a wedding present. And I've got that all settled, too. Here's my idea, Mamie. Why don't we get together, you and I, and buy the newlyweds *that!* (*He stares dead-front.* AUNTIE MAME *follows his gaze, but doesn't see anything.*)

AUNTIE MAME: What?

MR. UPSON: Why, that lot—right next door. Wouldn't

that make a wedding present, though? We could take down this wall here so that their patio would come smack up against ours. You couldn't tell where one left off and the other began!

AUNTIE MAME: So you wouldn't really be losing a daughter: you'd be gaining a patio!

MR. UPSON: But we've got to move fast. Some people are bidding on that property. (*He lowers his voice.*) The *wrong* kind.

AUNTIE MAME: Oh?

MR. UPSON: Fella named Epstein. A-bra-ham Epstein.

AUNTIE MAME (*enthusing*): The cellist? How lucky you are. All that lovely music right next door! And she's a darling. One of the nicest—

MRS. UPSON (*confidentially*): I guess maybe you don't understand quite how it *is* up here, Mamie. But this section is restricted only up to our property line. So we feel we have an obligation to make sure that— well—*you* know.

MR. UPSON: Tell you what I'll do, Mame. I'll have my broker make a bid—and when it goes in escrow we'll just divvy it up, fifty-fifty. You won't have to worry about a thing.

(AUNTIE MAME *plants her glass on the bar with an irritated precision that is only a hint of the emotion repressed within her.*)

AUNTIE MAME (*too quietly*): My, you've thought of everything, haven't you! Laid out Patrick's career— planned the wedding—even chosen my wedding gift.

Well, I guess the only thing left for me is to give an intimate family dinner.

(*She puts out her hands in a gesture of gracious help-lessness.*)

MR. UPSON: Fine!

MRS. UPSON (*blindly gulping the hook*): What a lovely idea, Mamie. I'll look in Gloria's book and give you a date.

AUNTIE MAME: Good. And why don't we invite Dwight, Claude? He's really part of the family, isn't he?

MRS. UPSON: That *would* be nice.

MR. UPSON: Well, Mamie, I've got only one thing to say to you, old girl. You're *top-hole!* (AUNTIE MAME *lowers her eyes modestly.* MR. UPSON *refills his own glass.*) Well, here's to *our* Glory . . . and *our* Patrick.

MRS. UPSON: And may the kiddies always be as happy as *we* are right now.

AUNTIE MAME (*lifting the glass, but looking a little ill*): At least.

(*The lights fade.*)

*The Beekman Place apartment. The room is under-
going another metamorphosis, and any previous
decor would seem definitely mid-Victorian. The
panels have been reversed to display some Fauvist
outrages. The furniture looks like a geometrist's
nightmare. But presiding over this transformation
is a trim redhead named* PEGEEN RYAN, *who is crisp
and businesslike as she arranges the abstract ashtrays
and the Twenty-First-century objets d'art.*

At first, PEGEEN *is bustling about the apartment
alone. Then* AGNES GOOCH *enters from right. She, too,
has been transformed by the miracle of maternity.
There is no doubt about it; the* GOOCH *is six months
pregnant. Her pelvis protests at every step as she
crosses wordlessly to the kitchen. Neither* GOOCH *nor*
PEGEEN *pays the slightest attention to the other.*
GOOCH *goes off.* PATRICK, *in dinner dress, appears in
the foyer and lets himself in. His nervousness gives*

way to amazement as he enters and takes in the new decor.

PATRICK: What's going on?

PEGEEN: Face lifting. (*She sizes up* PATRICK, *not uncritically.*) You must be the heir apparent. The "Little Love."

PATRICK (*wandering around the room*): Are you the new decorator? Did you do all this?

PEGEEN (*grins*): For money. (ITO *enters in livery, carrying the bare skeleton of a futuristic sofa.*) Right here, Ito. That's fine.

(ITO *puts down the sofa at* PEGEEN'S *direction.*)

PATRICK: What are you made up for, Ito? Where's my aunt?

ITO: Missy dress now. (ITO *goes off.*)

(PEGEEN *gathers up some cushions and places them on the bench.*)

PATRICK: What's that?

PEGEEN: It's a sofa. Danish Modern. You find it every place except Denmark. Your Aunt made it very explicit: she said she didn't want a sofa that sat around singing "Nearer My God to Thee."

PATRICK: Yeah, but do *you* like it?

PEGEEN: She's not paying me to like it. If she told me she wanted a tombstone for a coffee table, I'd get her a tombstone for a coffee table. And it would be a *good* tombstone. But that doesn't mean I'm going out and buy one for myself.

PATRICK: You should have told my aunt that.

PEGEEN: I did.

PATRICK: You know, you're the first *honest* interior decorator she's ever had, Miss . . . ?

PEGEEN: Pegeen Ryan. Unincorporated.

PATRICK (*shaking her hand, pleasantly*): Hi.

PEGEEN: Hi.

> (*But* PATRICK *is restless again. He glances toward the head of the stairs.*)

PATRICK: Where is she? Where's my aunt?

PEGEEN: You already asked that.

PATRICK: Did I?

PEGEEN: Relax. People get married every day.

PATRICK (*nervously*): I'm not getting married every day. I'm getting married three weeks from Tuesday.

PEGEEN (*tossing it off*): Congratulations.

AUNTIE MAME: Patrick—!

> (*He turns and sees* AUNTIE MAME *starting down the stairs. She is really dressed to the hilt, in a gold hostess gown. Both she and* PATRICK *start speaking at once.*)

PATRICK: Auntie Mame, what's the idea of all this?

AUNTIE MAME (*anticipating his protest*): Now, Patrick, I don't want to hear a word out of you. I simply *had* to drive up to Mountebank. Doris insisted!

PATRICK: Oh, that part's all right—they adore you. (*Casting a dubious eye around the room.*) But why did you have to change—?

AUNTIE MAME (*innocently*): Really, I'm so relieved. Now,

I've tried to make everything special for tonight, and
to give the Upsons as cozy a time as they gave me.

(PATRICK *nods vaguely.* PEGEEN *crosses briskly toward
the coffee table.*)

PAGEEN: Oh, I could only get two of these fetus-shaped
ashtrays. (*She indicates two ceramic receptacles guar-
anteed to give a jolt even to a smoker of Parlia-
ments. But* AUNTIE MAME *looks at them lovingly.*)

AUNTIE MAME: *Twins!* Aren't they dear? (*She arranges
them side by side on the coffee table, then steps back
to admire the effect.*)

PATRICK (*a little worried*): Yeah.

PEGEEN (*suddenly*): Oh! I forgot the horror!

(PEGEEN *darts off right, but* AUNTIE MAME *calls after
her.*)

AUNTIE MAME: Don't say that, Pegeen. It gives a surge
and flow to the whole room.

PATRICK: You mean there's more?

(PEGEEN *is off.* AUNTIE MAME *addresses* PATRICK
eagerly.)

AUNTIE MAME: It's divine. Wait till you see it! Damnedest
thing I ever bought! (*She parts her skirt, revealing
chic slacks underneath.*)

PATRICK (*wincing at her profanity*): Uh—Auntie Mame,
I don't suppose it's really necessary to say this—but
with Gloria's folks, I hope you won't let your lan-
guage get too—well, too *vivid*.

AUNTIE MAME: I won't use one teensy-weensy son-of-a-bitch all evening.

PATRICK: Good. And one other little thing. Politically, I guess you gathered they're on the conservative side.

AUNTIE MAME: I'm only wearing Republican clothes.

PEGEEN'S VOICE (*calling from off*): Could somebody give me a hand with the ladder?

AUNTIE MAME: Patrick, be a little gentleman and help Pegeen, will you?

PATRICK (*agreeably, as he exits right*): Yeah. Sure.

(AGNES GOOCH *emerges from the kitchen, munching a canapé.*)

AUNTIE MAME: Mustn't nibble on the hors d'oeuvres, Agnes. You'll get fat.

GOOCH: I'm sorry, Mrs. Burnside. I try to do exactly what you say. You're so wonderful. Nobody else would have taken me in my hour of need. I'll never be able to thank you.

AUNTIE MAME: Oh, twaddle—I'm the grateful one. You've given me a new interest—someone to look after, now that I'm losing Patrick.

GOOCH: I wish *I* had somebody to look after.

AUNTIE MAME: You will, dear, you will.

(GOOCH *is dragging herself up the stairs as* PATRICK *backs through the door right, helping* PEGEEN *with the stepladder. He doesn't see the pregnant secretary, who stops halfway up the stairs to watch.* PEGEEN *is carrying a tasteful but bizarre mobile.*)

PATRICK (*to* PEGEEN): Where do you want me to set this up?

PEGEEN: Right where you are is fine.

(PATRICK *unfolds the ladder, and* PEGEEN *starts up it to hang the mobile in place.* PATRICK *looks at it warily.*)

PATRICK: What's that supposed to be, anyway?

AUNTIE MAME (*quickly*): You don't like it.

PATRICK: Well, it might be a little *avant-garde* for the Upsons.

AUNTIE MAME (*decisively*): Pegeen, take it right down. I want everything to be absolutely perfect for Patrick.

(PEGEEN *hesitates at the top of the ladder.*)

GOOCH (*from halfway up the stairs*): *I* think it's very unusual.

(PATRICK *wheels around as if he'd been stabbed.*)

PATRICK: What the hell is Agnes doing here?

AUNTIE MAME (*innocently*): Where else would she be in her friendless condition?

PATRICK: This is one thing the Upsons simply will not understand.

AUNTIE MAME: We don't have to talk about it. Maybe they won't notice.

PATRICK: Won't notice! (GOOCH *whimpers on the staircase. In the outer hallway* MR. *and* MRS. UPSON *and* GLORIA *appear and ring the buzzer.*) (*Panicked.*) My God— they're here!

PEGEEN (*from the ladder*): Help me get this thing down!

PATRICK (*hastily*): No, no—leave it up! Just get the ladder out of here!

AUNTIE MAME: Norah—Ito—somebody, answer the door.

GOOCH (*helpfully, starting down the stairs*): I'll get it.

(PATRICK *leaps toward the staircase to block her.*)

PATRICK: Oh, no you don't!

AUNTIE MAME: Now, now, Agnes, Patrick is right. (*Firmly.*) I want you to go upstairs and *stay* there.

GOOCH: What'll I *do*, Mrs. Burnside?

AUNTIE MAME: *Sleep*, Agnes! Knit! Read Dr. Gesell. (*The door buzzes again, a little more impatiently. With painful slowness, GOOCH starts up the stairs again. As PEGEEN folds the ladder and disappears with it, ITO scampers out of the kitchen and opens the door for the UPSONS. AUNTIE MAME extends her hands in greeting.*) Welcome, welcome to the Burnside fireside!

MR. UPSON: Good to see you, Mamie! You don't look a day older. (*He laughs.*)

AUNTIE MAME: Doris—and little Glory! How I've been looking forward to this evening.

GLORIA (*the well-bred robot*): I can't tell you how pleased I am to see you again.

(MRS. UPSON *looks around, a little baffled by the decor.*)

MRS. UPSON: My!

PATRICK: Hi, everybody. Glory.

AUNTIE MAME: Do sit down. (*The UPSONS settle down in the furniture, with some difficulty. MRS. UPSON, who is no Channel swimmer, finds herself with her knees high in the air and her buttocks in the nap of the rug.*) Are you perfectly comfortable down there, Doris?

MRS. UPSON: Oh, it's so *interesting!*

AUNTIE MAME: Now, I know you're all just perishing for something to drink after that long drive down the parkway. (*Calling.*) Ito, bring in the punch!

PATRICK: Punch?

(MR. BABCOCK *has appeared in the outer hallway, and rings the buzzer.* ITO *comes out, carrying a tray with a dozen or so curious, torch-shaped glasses. At the sound of the buzzer, he passes the punch bowl and glasses to* NORAH, *who has entered behind him.* ITO *scampers to the door and admits* BABCOCK. NORAH *passes glasses to each guest.*

In counterpoint to MR. BABCOCK'S *entrance,* GLORIA *looks up at the mobile, quizzically.*)

GLORIA: What's that *thing* hanging there?

PATRICK (*without affectation*): It's an abstraction. Non-representational.

GLORIA (*girly-girly to* AUNTIE MAME): Mrs. Burnside, how'm I ever going to stop this nephew of yours from using such big words!

MR. UPSON (*as he spies* MR. BABCOCK *in the door*): Dwight!

MR. BABCOCK: Claude!

(MR. UPSON *tries to get up to shake hands, but is having some difficulty getting out of the low furniture.*)

AUNTIE MAME: How good of you to come, Mr. Babcock.

(NORAH *has put the silver tray down on the bar, and*
AUNTIE MAME *is ladling out drinks into the torchlike
glasses.*

MR. BABCOCK, *moving to shake hands with* MR. UPSON,
crashes into the mobile.)

MR. BABCOCK: Ooops.

AUNTIE MAME: Oh dear, we'll have to raise that. (*Calling.*)
Pegeen, would you bring back the ladder? (*She stops*
MR. UPSON *from drinking.*) Won't you sit down, Mr.
Babcock. Now, they're almost ready—the *specialité
de la maison.* (PEGEEN *re-enters with the ladder.*) I'm
afraid you'll have to get that a little higher, dear; it's
getting in people's hair. (PEGEEN *sets up the ladder
and climbs up to adjust the mobile.*) Oh, I want you
all to meet Miss Pegeen Ryan.

MRS. UPSON: Are you the aircraft Ryans?

PEGEEN: Afraid not—just the bricklaying Ryans.

AUNTIE MAME: Claude, I'm not going to tell you one
thing that's in these drinks—because *all* the ingre-
dients are secret. (*She takes a long Japanese kindling
match from the table.*) Now, hold still! (*She sets fire
to the drink in* MR. UPSON'S *hand.*)

MR. UPSON (*a little stunned*): Well, what do you know!

(AUNTIE MAME *moves from guest to guest, igniting the
drinks.*)

AUNTIE MAME: The trick is to drink them up fast, before
all the alcohol burns away. (*She lights another drink
for* PEGEEN *on the ladder.*)

PEGEEN: I feel like Miss Liberty.

(PATRICK *seems a little surprised that* AUNTIE MAME *has included* PEGEEN *in the party, but he doesn't say anything.*

Each of the guests holds his drink at arm's length. They make abortive attempts to bring the glasses close to their faces, but the heat makes them thrust the torches away again.)

AUNTIE MAME: A dear friend of mine who may drop in later calls this "The Flaming Mame."

PATRICK (*tensing up again*): Who? Who? who's dropping in later?

AUNTIE MAME: Just family, Patrick. (PATRICK *looks a little like the captain of the* Titanic *just after he talked to the boiler room.* MRS. UPSON *makes an attempt to sip her drink, but withdraws suddenly—and bats at her eyebrows as if trying to extinguish a small conflagration.*) Why, don't be an old 'fraidy-cat, Doris! There's nothing to be scared of; we're fully covered by fire insurance. (*She slaps* MR. UPSON *on the shoulder, knowing he will appreciate the wisdom of this.*) Now, are we all lit?

PATRICK (*restlessly*): Mr. Upson, wouldn't you be happier if I fixed you a daiquiri?

MR. UPSON: No, no, son. Not for a minute. Your auntie fixed this for me, and I'm going to drink it. Why, it looks just *fine*.

(NORAH *and* ITO *come out bearing an elaborate tray of hors d'oeuvres.*)

GLORIA (*nibbling on one of the hors d'oeuvres*): Oh, this is spicy! Try one of the little striped ones, Mums.

(*Delightedly* ITO *and* NORAH *pass "the little striped ones" to all the guests. Deftly* AUNTIE MAME *declines.*)

MR. BABCOCK: Say, these *are* tasty.

MRS. UPSON (*to* AUNTIE MAME): What are they, dear?

AUNTIE MAME: Just plain old pickled rattlesnake. (*The process of mastication ceases instantly.* GLORIA *goes into a paroxysm of coughing. Helpfully* AUNTIE MAME *tries to force one of the flaming drinks into* GLORIA'S *hand.*) Why, it's pure protein. And before they marinate them, they *always* remove the fangs. Mr. Babcock, you've gone out!

(*The perfect hostess, she moves to relight his drink.*)

MR. BABCOCK (*waving her aside*): Don't bother, Mrs. Burnside.

(AUNTIE MAME *looks hurt.*)

MRS. UPSON: Mamie, dear, with the wedding only three weeks away, I've just got to decide. Would you say six bridesmaids?

GLORIA: Muriel Puce had eight.

AUNTIE MAME: Then I'd say let's keep up with the Puces.

(*The bedroom door opens and* AGNES GOOCH *waddles down the stairs.* PATRICK *turns the color of skim milk.* AUNTIE MAME *addresses* GOOCH *as if she were a puppy who had just been indiscreet on a new carpet.*) Agnes, I told you to *stay in your room!*

GOOCH (*whining helplessly*): But, Mrs. Burnside, it's a quarter past eight. And you told me . . .

AUNTIE MAME (*quickly*): I told you to *take your pills* at a quarter past eight.

GOOCH: But my calcium pills are in the kitchen.

PATRICK: Auntie Mame!

(GOOCH *painfully makes her way down the stairs, and all eyes are on her. It would be easier to conceal an elephant in Bergdorf's window. No effort is made to introduce or explain* GOOCH, *which makes the pause all the more painful and telling.*)

MR. UPSON (*leaning over to* MR. BABCOCK, *confidentially*): Is that a member of the family?

MR. BABCOCK: Damned if I know.

MR. UPSON: It's a member of *some*body's family.

AUNTIE MAME (*making the best of it*): Doris, I'd like you to meet my secretary. She's a little bit—she's not quite her*self* at the moment.

MRS. UPSON (*warmly, to the* GOOCH): Now, we know all about these *women's* things, don't we! (*Sympathetically.*) What's your name, dear?

GOOCH (*simpers*): Gooch.

MRS. UPSON (*taking her arm*): You sit right over here beside me, Mrs. Gooch. (AUNTIE MAME *and* PATRICK *exchange a glance. When* GOOCH *sits in this modern furniture, she really spreads.*) A little expectant mother always makes me feel weepy. I remember when I was carrying Gloria.

GLORIA: Oh, Mummy.

(GOOCH *reaches over and takes a canapé.*)

AUNTIE MAME (*warning*): Now, now, Agnes—

MRS. UPSON: Remember, Mamie—she's eating for two. (*Turns back to* GOOCH.) And what does *Mr.* Gooch do?

GOOCH: Oh, my father passed on.

MRS. UPSON: Oh, no, I mean your husband.

(GOOCH *lets out a protracted wail. Both* PATRICK *and* AUNTIE MAME *have descended on her and are helping her out of the sofa from either side.*)

AUNTIE MAME (*singing it out*): Calcium time! Pegeen!

(*With* PEGEEN's *help, the* GOOCH *is steered off into the kitchen.*

PATRICK *turns back to face the guests, sweating.*)

PATRICK: You know, there's one thing about my Auntie Mame. She's *bighearted;* whenever anybody's in trouble, she—

(*The doorbell buzzes.*

PATRICK *jumps.* ITO *goes to the door, opens it, and ushers in* VERA CHARLES, *dripping foxes, as usual.*)

AUNTIE MAME (*effusively*): Vera!

VERA: Mame, darling. Like an opening night—without critics! Heaven!

(MRS. UPSON *nudges* MR. UPSON.)

MRS. UPSON (*lowering her voice somewhat, excitedly*): Claude! Claude! That's Vera Charles, the famous actress, just as sure as I'm sitting here.

AUNTIE MAME: Mr. and Mrs. Upson, Miss Upson, Mr. Babcock—I want you to meet my dearest friend, Vera Charles.

MRS. UPSON (*under her breath*): I told you, Claude, I told you!

(VERA *quickly senses that this is a matinee house.*)

VERA (*turning it on*): How do you do. I'm so charmed to meet you, all of you.

GLORIA (*rushing up*): Miss Charles, I've just got to tell you how I *adored* you in *End of Summer*.

VERA (*with a frozen smile*): Did you, dear? That was Ina Claire.

AUNTIE MAME: Vera, can I persuade you to have a drink?

VERA: Oh, yes. Anything but rum! I've just been at the most God-awful party, and all they had were daiquiris—made with *honey* yet!! (*She makes a grimace and pours herself a tumbler of straight Scotch.*)

(*The doorbell chimes and* ITO *ushers in the slightly grayed but still muscular figure of* RALPH DEVINE.)

AUNTIE MAME: Ralph Devine! You're a *dream* to come.

(PATRICK *turns away with a cramp in his solar plexus.*)

PATRICK: Oh, God!

AUNTIE MAME: Doris, you were considerate enough to show me the pictures of your little Gloria's school-teachers—Miss Tuthill and all that mob—and I thought you'd like to meet Patrick's very *first* school-teacher here in New York.

RALPH (*blandly*): Why, Mame, don't you have a picture of me?

AUNTIE MAME (*easily*): Not one we could show in mixed company.

(*There are some eyebrows cocked at this, but* RALPH *floats effortlessly among the guests for introductions. He wears a skin-tight jersey sport shirt that is open at the neck not quite to the navel. He looks at* MR. BABCOCK *curiously.*)

RALPH: Say, haven't we met somewhere before?

MR. BABCOCK (*studying him narrowly*): I don't recognize the *face*.

MR. UPSON (*leaning forward and picking up one of the ashtrays from the coffee table*): You know, the first time I looked at this ashtray, I thought it was— (*Shocked.*) My God, it *is*!

PATRICK: Auntie Mame, I thought it was going to be just family tonight.

AUNTIE MAME: But you don't want the Upsons to think we don't have any friends. After all, these are the people who helped raise you. (*Glancing up at* PEGEEN, *who seems to be having trouble with the mobile.*) Are you having trouble, Pegeen? (*Turning.*) Patrick, why don't you give her a hand?

MRS. UPSON (*holding the ashtray*): But, Claude, it couldn't be.

UPSON: You've got it upside down.

(PATRICK *starts up the ladder to help* PEGEEN. *When*

he gets to the top, he is in fairly close juxtaposition to PEGEEN, *and* GLORIA *is not very much pleased.*)

PEGEEN (*nearly losing her balance*): Ohhhhhhh! (PATRICK *throws his arms around her to keep her from falling. She grins at him.*) Thanks, Lochinvar.

PATRICK (*smiling back*): Courtesy of the house.

PEGEEN: I'm okay. You've got troubles enough of your own.

PATRICK: Don't I, though?

GLORIA (*indignant*): Well, that's a pretty picture, I *must* say!

(VERA *decides it's time for her to go on, and she takes center stage, as usual.*)

VERA: Yes. Isn't it? Ladies and gentlemen, I want to propose a toast. (*She lifts her glass toward* PEGEEN *and* PATRICK *at the top of the ladder.*) To this lovely young couple, as they start up the ladder of life together.

PATRICK (*coming down the ladder hastily*): No, no, Auntie Vera—*this* isn't Gloria, *that's* Gloria.

(VERA *turns and finds herself staring straight into the frozen visage of* GLORIA UPSON.)

VERA: Pity. (VERA *downs her Scotch.*)

(*The door buzzer rings.* ITO *moves to the door.*

PEGEEN *has succeeded in hanging the mobile but is too fascinated by this three-ring circus to descend from her grandstand seat atop the ladder.*

LINDSAY *comes in, carrying a thick manila envelope.*)

AUNTIE MAME (*crossing to greet him*): Lindsay, Lindsay—that's what we've needed—calm, reasonable you.

LINDSAY (*smiling proudly*): I hope I'm not crashing in on anything, Mame, but I couldn't wait. I had to bring it right over.

AUNTIE MAME: What is it?

(*Pleased,* LINDSAY *hands her the envelope.*)

LINDSAY: Be careful—the ink's still wet.

(AUNTIE MAME *draws out of the envelope the galley proofs of her book.*)

AUNTIE MAME: My book!

LINDSAY: Mame, you'll have to correct these galleys; it's your last chance to change your life.

AUNTIE MAME (*jubilantly waving the galleys*): Look, everybody! I'm in print—just like Fannie Hurst!

(VERA *crosses to* AUNTIE MAME *and takes some of the galleys from her, looking at them interestedly.*)

PATRICK: Congratulations, Auntie Mame.

(PATRICK *crosses to* AUNTIE MAME *and she puts her arm around him warmly.*)

AUNTIE MAME: Darling, I hope you don't mind, there is a lot in here about you. (*She hands him a fistful of the galleys.*)

MR. UPSON: Well, this seems to be quite a day for you, Mamie.

MRS. UPSON: An authoress! Well!

GLORIA: Patrick, you old meanie!—Why didn't you tell us your auntie was *some*body.

RALPH (*crossing to* AUNTIE MAME): Am I mentioned in your book, Mame?

AUNTIE MAME: Mentioned! You're *exposed!*

(*She hands him some of the galleys to peruse. In fact, everybody is busy going through the galleys, except the* UPSONS *and* MR. BABCOCK, *who seem definitely on the outside and nonparticipants in this activity.*)

VERA: You know, I've been to so many wonderful parties here, Mame. Now I'm going to find out how they all ended.

PATRICK (*laughing warmly as he reads one of the galleys*): Hey, I'd almost forgotten about the time we got locked in the Mummy Room at the Metropolitan. (*He flips to another galley.*) And the time you got Miss Earhart to give me a flying lesson. (*He laughs.*) Boy, I had no talent for *that!* (*He flips to another galley. Warmly.*) And here's all about the roller skates. And Uncle Beau. And that Christmas when we were so broke . . .

(*They laugh reminiscently. Suddenly* GLORIA *claims the center of attention.*)

GLORIA: Mrs. Burnside, you could practically write a whole book about what happened to *me*.

(*But through the babble of conversation,* AUNTIE MAME *didn't quite hear what* GLORIA *said.*)

AUNTIE MAME: I beg your pardon, Gloria?

GLORIA: I said, you could practically write a whole book about what happened to me. (*Everyone quiets down to listen to* GLORIA's *narrative, which she dramatizes athletically.*) Bunny Bixler and I were in the semifinals—the very semifinals, mind you—of the ping-pong tournament at the club, and this *ghastly* thing happened. We were both playing way over our heads, and the score was 29-28, and we had this terrific volley, and I ran back to get this really terrific shot . . . (*She runs back, demonstrating with an imaginary ping-pong paddle—then stops like Lady Macbeth.*) . . . and I *stepped* on the ping-pong ball! Just squashed it to nothing! And then Bunny and I went to the closet of the game room to get another ping-pong ball, and the closet was *locked!* Imagine! So we had to call the whole thing off. It was ghastly, just ghastly!

(*There is another dazed pause.* VERA *screws a fresh drink into* AUNTIE MAME's *numbed hand, and turns her attention back to the galleys.*)

MRS. UPSON (*with a forced chuckle*): But it *is* amusing!

MR. BABCOCK: Yes. It is amusing.

VERA: It's hilarious!

AUNTIE MAME (*startled*): *What* is?

VERA (*deep in the galleys*): *Your* story.

LINDSAY: And the most important thing, Vera, is that she did it all by herself. There isn't an Alana or a Cocca maura in the whole book.

(GOOCH *enters from the kitchen.*

VERA, *whose joints have now been loosened by an alcoholic oiling, crosses to the Upsons.*)

VERA (*confidentially*): You know, you'll never believe this, Mr. Upjohn, but Lindsay got this Irish slob— Brian . . . what was his name? Oh, it doesn't matter —to come here and live with Mame till she got the book finished. Of course, he didn't do a damn thing except—(*She breaks off, fortunately.*) Mame, my hat's off to you!

(AGNES GOOCH *has been lured to the galleys, and her voice cracks as she makes an emotional announcement from the staircase.*)

GOOCH (*ecstatically*): I'm so proud! The whole last chapter is about *me!* (*She reads.*) "Fighting the stigma of the unwed mother!" (*She flattens out on the stairs to read.*)

(*Now the* UPSONS *and* BABCOCK *are shocked to the marrow.*)

MR. BABCOCK (*trying to soothe the irate* UPSONS): Claude, as soon as we get him away from the aunt, everything's going to be fine.

VERA (*reading galleys*): Why, Patrick, I never realized how many times you unzipped me and put me to bed!

(*There is much good-natured laughter at this, but* MR. UPSON *takes on a righteous tone.*)

MR. UPSON (*standing, piously*): Now, just a moment. We have some *young* people here.

PATRICK (*trying to gloss it over*): Well, sir, I only did it when Miss Charles passed out!

(*This, of course, makes it worse; the* UPSONS *are certain that* AUNTIE MAME'S *apartment is a den of iniquity.*)

GLORIA: Patrick, how can you defend people who—who—

PATRICK (*acidly*): Who've never played ping-pong?

GLORIA (*haughtily to* PATRICK): I certainly hope when we're married you won't invite people like *this* to our house!

PATRICK: Who *is* coming to our house—Muriel Puce and Bunny Bixler?

GLORIA (*regally*): What's wrong with Muriel Puce?

PATRICK: Nothing, not a damned thing! Except she's got the I.Q. of a dead flashlight battery!

GLORIA: *Well!*

VERA (*dramatically*): Lindsay, it's marvelous. Mame's going to make a fortune from this book!

LINDSAY: She sure as hell will. But not for herself. Mame's assigned all of her royalties to the Epstein Home in Mountebank.

RALPH (*interested*): Epstein the cellist?

MR. UPSON: What? What's that about Mountebank?

VERA: Can't the Epsteins afford their own home?

AUNTIE MAME: No, Vera, they're not going to *live* there. They're building a home for refugee Jewish children.

(*There is a warm and favorable reaction from* MAME'S *inner circle.*)

MR. UPSON (*frigidly*): Are you ready, Doris?

MRS. UPSON: I've been ready for quite a long time.

MR. UPSON: Come, Glory. We have a long way to go. (*He starts herding them toward the door.*)

BABCOCK: Claude, please! Claude! (*Shaken,* BABCOCK *strides back into the room. He explodes vehemently directly at* AUNTIE MAME.) For nine years, Mame Dennis Burnside, I've done everything I could to protect this boy from your cockeyed, idiotic nincompoopery! But this is the limit. Now you've ruined everything—all my plans for this boy's future—

(PATRICK *has turned away, and* AUNTIE MAME *reaches with her eyes to see how he has taken all of this.*)

AUNTIE MAME (*to* BABCOCK): Your plans, your plans! You have the bill of fare, and you're shouting orders for everybody. (*Lowers her voice.*) But did it ever occur to you that this boy might be hungry for something that you never even heard of? (*Softening.*) When Patrick walked into my life—a frightened little boy hanging onto Norah's hand—it was love at first sight. For nine years I've tried to open some windows in his life. (*She turns on* BABCOCK.) Now all you want to do is shut him up in some—(*She reaches for the appropriate word.*)—some safe-deposit box. Well, I won't let you do that to my little one! (*She stops abruptly, distantly.*) No. He's not little any more. And he's not mine. But he's not yours either, Mr. Babcock. I doubt very much that Patrick will allow you to settle him down in some dry-veined, restricted community. Make him an Aryan from Darien!—and marry him off to a girl with *braces on her brains!*

(AUNTIE MAME *stands there, breathless, triumphant.*

BABCOCK *exits.*

LINDSAY *crosses to* MAME, *narrowing his eyes slightly.*)

LINDSAY: Mame, did you deliberately *plan* all this?

AUNTIE MAME (*looking at him innocently*): Don't be ridiculous, Lindsay. You know Patrick always makes all his own decisions. (PATRICK *looks at his aunt with a crooked smile;* MAME, *ever the hostess, takes the center of the room with a tray of canapés.*) Rattlesnake, anyone?

PATRICK (*to* MAME, *warmly*): Thank you, Lady Iris.

AUNTIE MAME: Charmed, Lord Dudley. (*And perhaps there are tears in her eyes.*)

(*The lights fade.*)

Immediately following AUNTIE MAME'S *party, we hear the choral voices singing a bizarre variant on Rimsky-Korsakov's "Song of India."*

AUNTIE MAME'S VOICE: Oh, sahib, sahib, will you help me with this cablegram, please? Oh, where am I?

INDIAN VOICE: Punjab, India.

AUNTIE MAME'S VOICE: June 28, 19——. What year is it?

INDIAN VOICE: 1946.

(Exactly as at the beginning of the play, there is a projection on the scrim. AUNTIE MAME'S *voice is heard over the loudspeaker as the words unfold.)*

AUNTIE MAME *(voice offstage)*: Mr. and Mrs. Patrick Dennis, 224 East 50th Street, New York.

Dear Patrick and Pegeen. Arriving from India June thirty-first. Please meet me Beekman Place apartment. Uncle Lindsay off on safari with Maharani. Means nothing.

Coming back to pick up nylons, Nescafe, Kleenex, and dentures for Maharani.

Only staying two days. Will explain why when I see you, because cable rates are ninety rupees per word and obviously only a damned fool would be silly enough to waste all the money on a long cablegram that went on and on and on and on. . . .

(*Her voice fades as the projection fades.*

We bleed through the scrim to see PATRICK *and* PEGEEN *pacing the Beekman Place apartment. The scrim flies.*

A tiger skin, some elephant tusks, and some packing boxes are scattered about.)

PAT (*calling toward off right*): Auntie Mame, what are you doing in there?

AUNTIE MAME (*entering*): Just giving Michael his presents, dear.

(MICHAEL *comes on holding a turban.* MAME *is like an Indian princess in a flowing blue-green sari.*)

MICHAEL: Look, Dad! (*To* AUNTIE MAME.) Which is the front, Auntie Mame?

AUNTIE MAME: Let me do it for you, my little love. (*She puts the turban on him.*) There. Now salaam to your mother, Michael—like Auntie Mame just taught you. (MICHAEL *bows.*) Ahhh, very good, sahib.

PEGEEN: That's not a real sword, it it?

MICHAEL: It's a scimitar.

AUNTIE MAME (*looking at her watch*): Oh, dear! "Bell darwazay pair carr-ay ahn."

PATRICK: That's what I always say.

AUNTIE MAME: In Hindustani, that means, "The water oxen are waiting at the gate." Of course, *my* ox is waiting at Idlewild. Pan American Flight one hundred for Karachi. (*Turns back to* MICHAEL.) Oh, Michael, if I could only show you India! The splendor, the mystery, the elephants in the streets.

PATRICK: Now, Auntie Mame.

AUNTIE MAME: I know. I shouldn't even bring up the possibility of Michael's going to India with me.

MICHAEL: But Auntie Mame said she'd love to have me, she said so right in there.

PEGEEN: It's ridiculous. I wouldn't hear of it.

MICHAEL (*he turns to his father*): Dad?

PATRICK: Now look, it's out of the question completely. You heard your mother.

(MICHAEL *wheels on his mother.*)

MICHAEL (*earnestly*): You know what your trouble is, Mom? You don't live, live, *live!* Life is a banquet, and most poor sons-of-bitches are starving to death!

(PEGEEN *grabs* MICHAEL, *clamps her hand over his mouth, and holds him protectively.* AUNTIE MAME *and* PATRICK *exchange a significant glance.* PATRICK *crosses toward* MICHAEL *and* PEGEEN. PEGEEN *knows that in this family you live it up to the hilt—and there's no sense in trying to resist.*

Helplessly, PEGEEN *lets* MICHAEL *go.* PATRICK *steers him into the erratic but inspiring custody of* AUNTIE MAME.)

PEGEEN (*a little helplessly*): One thing you've got to understand. School begins the day after Labor Day. He's got to be back by then.

AUNTIE MAME (*vaguely*): Naturally. Of course. Labor Day. That's sometime in November, isn't it?

PATRICK (*firmly*): The first week in September, Auntie Mame.

MICHAEL (*taking* MAME's *hand*): Don't you worry, Dad. I'll be back by Labor Day.

AUNTIE MAME: Labor! Oh, the problem of labor in India is gargantuan.

MICHAEL: What's "gargantuan," Auntie Mame?

AUNTIE MAME: On the plane, Michael, I'll give you a pad and pencil, and you can write down all the words you don't understand. (AUNTIE MAME *draws* MICHAEL *toward the stairs and they start climbing*.) Come, darling. I've been out all morning shopping for your traveling gear. Let's go try things on. (*Continuing to climb*.) Oh, I'm going to open doors for you, Michael, doors you never dreamed even existed!

(MICHAEL *looks up at* AUNTIE MAME *adoringly*.)

PEGEEN: My God, she's the Pied Piper!

AUNTIE MAME: Oh, what times we're going to have, my little love. What vistas we're going to explore together. First we'll see the Taj Mahal—

(THEY *go off together toward that adventure of life, and we know what a banquet it is going to be for both of them*.)

The curtain falls.